03 10

CENTRAL
PA

D1110193

A BRADFOR

Fashionista

DISCARDED

MICOL OSTOW

SIMON PULSE
NEW YORK LONDON TORONTO SYDNEY

Thanks as ever to Liz, Andra, and Anica,
for endless patience and encouragement with this manuscript;
to Noah, for loving me even when I am deadline-crazed and hopped up on coffee
and Gummi Bears; to the Vermont College folks and especially Louise Hawes;
to Jodi Reamer; and, of course, to my friends and family

This book is a work of fiction. Any references to historical events,
real people, or real locales are used fictitiously. Other names, characters,
places, and incidents are the product of the author's imagination,
and any resemblance to actual events or locales or persons,
living or dead, is entirely coincidental.

SIMON PULSE
An imprint of Simon & Schuster Children's Publishing Division
1230 Avenue of the Americas, New York, NY 10020
First Simon Pulse paperback edition August 2009
Copyright © 2009 by FlirtyGirl Productions, LLC
All rights reserved, including the right of reproduction in whole or in part in any form.
SIMON PULSE and colophon are registered trademarks of Simon & Schuster, Inc.

Produced by FlirtyGirl Productions, LLC
1739 Lombard Street, Philadelphia, PA 19146

For information about special discounts for bulk purchases, please contact Simon & Schuster
Special Sales at 1-866-506-1949 or business@simonandschuster.com.
The Simon & Schuster Speakers Bureau can bring authors to your live event. For more
information or to book an event contact the Simon & Schuster Speakers Bureau at
1-866-248-3049 or visit our website at www.simonspeakers.com.
Book design by Lili Schwartz
The text of this book was set in Trade Gothic.
Manufactured in the United States of America
2 4 6 8 10 9 7 5 3 1
Library of Congress Control Number 2009923496
ISBN: 978-1-4169-6119-2

MASSAPEQUA PUBLIC LIBRARY

3 1616 00893 2762

*To all those folks out there in the
blogosphere—writers, readers, and other
assorted friendlies—who keep me
company while I work.
Who says writing is a solitary profession?*

CENTRAL' AVENUE
PAPER BACK
COLLECTION

Massapequa Public Library
523 Central Avenue
Massapequa, NY 11758
(516) 798-4607

DEMCO

Madison_Ave: is all kinds of *haute* and bothered.

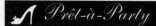 *Prêt-à-Party*

12/7, 3:11 a.m.
privacy setting: private collection

LOOSE LIPS

I have to say: I am certainly no stranger to drama. But usually, it's of the variety that belongs to someone else. For instance, Paige. Getting dragged away in handcuffs.

Okay, I'll admit I didn't see this key event with my own eyes. Limos are *definitely* fun, but the tinted windows make it tough to keep up with the latest scandal. Especially when you're busy creating a private scandal of your own. I honestly can't believe what went down with Tyler and me tonight.

Bottom line: If someone's getting busted, I'm seriously glad it's not me. I totally couldn't handle this decimating my friendship with Spence. Girls like Paige come and go, but Spencers are forever.

Thank God for FrontPaige making headlines again. Looks like my secret is under wraps . . . for now, anyway.

location: the Closet
status: afterglowing—I can't help it! Squee! Sorry, Spencer!
dirty secrets: just the one. But it's a biggie. This could all end *very* badly. . . .

GoldenGirl: is second-guessing.

---

to: Madison_Ave@bradfordprep.com
from: GoldenGirl@bradfordprep.com
date: 12/7, 2:20 p.m.
re: Blogorrhea

Hi, friendly:

So . . . about last night.

Crazy, *n'est-ce pas*? Every time I blink, I see them carting Paige off in handcuffs. And that major-league stink-eye she was flashing my way. I had no idea that false eyelashes could be used so adroitly for the power of evil.

Anyhoo, I know Paige's comeuppance was a long time, er, comeupping, but it still felt sort of sudden. Rehab, thy name is Paige. Again.

I know I did the right thing. Jeremy says so too. And according to Reegs, Paige wasn't this far into the hard stuff the last time she was shipped off to Zephyr. So I guess she really needed the reality check. And yet.

I wouldn't mind if you agreed with me. In so many words. Sooner rather than later. Before I decide I was channeling my inner Paige a bit too much last night.

Meanwhile, ever see Toni's old blog post about the weekend at the Oceana? Kaylen just IM'd me about it. I mean, I'm sure it's nothing and I can't even believe I'm bringing it up—that weekend was ages ago, and so weird anyway—but her blog had a little thing about you . . . and Tyler . . . getting a little too friendly?

Stupid, right?

If Toni is so desperately needy for attention and dirt, couldn't she have come up with something better than that? This *is* Bradford, after all.

Anyway, it's so dumb. I thought I'd mention it and then we could laugh about how dumb it is. Because it is. Dumber than dumb.

Right?

Looking forward to hearing how right I am,

Spence

to: GoldenGirl@bradfordprep.com
from: Madison_Ave@bradfordprep.com
date: 12/7, 3:17 p.m.
re: Blogorrhea

Dah-ling:

I guess it's true what they say: A leopard never changes its spots. And a tigress always keeps her claws sharpened and at the ready.

I can't *believe* Toni posted that on her blog! Talk about making a mountain out of a moleskin clutch! She obvs doesn't understand that Tyler and I are just friends, and not in any Hollywood publicist, "they're just friends, but really they're secretly dating" sort of way. I mean, our whole crew is all jokey and flirty and friendly. *All* of us, *all* of the time. Gawd.

It's such a shame that Toni's never had a flirty conversation with a studly boy. She might be more understanding of the sitch if she had any experience with the opposite sex. Someone really ought to let that girl know that jealousy is *out* this season. And it doesn't do much for her complexion, either. (Envy is extremely sallow-making.) Concocting rumors just to get under our collective skin is, as you say, complete and utter dumbness.

Speaking of who was getting down with whom, let's talk about last night: Dalton and Camden Barrett—get a room, peeps! This is the Hollywood Ball, not Hollywood Boulevard! Did he even wait until Paige had been escorted from the premises before hunting down another hookup?

I know, I know: pot, kettle. I have become what I hate. I'll shut up now.

And no worries, you did the right thing re: Paige. I've been telling you for weeks that she was over the edge.

Meet you in the lounge tomorrow before first period?

Mwah!

Mads

---

to: Madison_Ave@bradfordprep.com
from: GoldenGirl@bradfordprep.com
date: 12/7, 5:03 p.m.
re: Friendliness

Miss Maddie:

I was obviously having a case of temporary insanity that I even bothered to ask the question. I should learn not to be so gullible. Thanks for not making a thing of it. You're the bestest (of course).

xx,

Spence

PS: Screw pots and kettles. I might need the gory deets on Cam and Dalton. For serious.

Madison_Ave: hearts gory deets. When they're not about her.

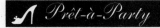

12/7, 7:52 p.m.
privacy setting: private collection

LIES OF THE WHITE VARIETY

Or, um, if not quite as white as the illegal substance that was found on Paige Andrews's person last night, then perhaps more of an ivory or an ecru. An eggshell, if you will. Much like those eggshells that I'll be walking on when I get near Spencer, if I don't watch myself.

So maybe I fibbed a little. But it's not as though I told Spencer a complete untruth. It was really more like a fiblette. I mean, yeah, so, Tyler and I have been *haute*-and-heavy with the flirting for a while now. I tried to ignore it, tried to pretend it didn't mean anything. I mean, he's my BFF's BF. Despite the flirtaliciousness, we didn't actually get seriously horizontal until the Hollywood Ball. And even then, it's not like we meant to do it or anything. It was mostly just drunken misbehavior. *In vino retarditas.* So to tell Spencer that nothing was going on back at Bar Fetish is to be strictly truthful.

I guess.

I hooked up with my best friend's boyfriend.

And also? I liked it.

Now my stomach is twisted into thorny knots. It feels like the time I ate three servings of original Smooch mojito gelato and then let C.J. drive me around Rittenhouse in his Audi R8. Kind of in a good way, kind of in a less good way.

I love Spencer. But *mmm*, whatever that was with Tyler . . . It's like the hummy sort of skin tingles that you get after a good, long sweat session in the sauna. And it's going to be pretty hard to go back to the way things used to be. To be honest, I don't know if I can. Flirtaliciousness may not be enough anymore.

No.

I won't put Spence-and-Mads in jeopardy. Not if I can help it. What was it I said before? *Spencers are forever.* I'm not going to risk our relationship for a little kissy-face with Tyler. Sauna-hummy skin tingles or no.

No way.

Not a chance.

Nope.

Not me.

Never.

location: the kitchen
status: whitewashed
resolved: to do the right thing. And bury my big-time mistake.

12/8, 9:00 p.m.
privacy setting: private collection

A CUT ABOVE

Actually, "cut" is such an ugly word. Let's just refer to it as a "calculated absence," shall we? Besides, it's not like gym counts as a real class. I mean, if Spencer and I give our coach a flash of thigh sometime next week, we're each guaranteed an A for the semester, I should think. Hence the last-period class missage by yours truly and her BFF.

Our reasoning was pretty solid: Spence's mom had flown in Geoffroy Grison, master skin technician, straight from the French Riviera. He has this new *poisson* pedicure process (fun with alliteration!) that apparently leaves your feet as smooth as a socialite's post-dermabrasion cheek. And we've both been feeling a touch raggedy of late. I mean, seeing your best frenemy carted off by the boys in blue? Stressful. Mrs. Kelly thought spa treatments would help mellow us out, and I was in full agreement.

Unfortunately, I hadn't given much thought to what a *poisson* pedi might entail.

Specifically, *les poisson.*

In plain English: fish.

"So, they, um . . . bite your feet off?"

I leveled Spencer with my best dubious gaze. Planting my feet in a basin filled with mini-piranhas did not exactly sound like the height of luxury. To be frank, the whole thing smacked of unhygienic danger. If Mrs. Kelly weren't behind it all, I would have run for the nearest available consultant at the Ritz-Carlton's Richel D'Ambra Spa.

"They do not 'bite your feet off,'" Spencer countered, perfectly plucked eyebrows twitching with impatience. "They exfoliate the calluses on your heels."

"With their *mouths*." My voice rose. "Their scaly, fishy little mouths." I've never thought of myself as fish-phobic—I practically live on sushi, after all—but then again, I've never seriously contemplated plunging my heels into a bowl of fish with the intention of having them ingest my dead skin cells either.

I shuddered.

From his setup in the sitting room, Geoffroy clucked to himself. I wondered if he'd had his *poisson* insured before that transatlantic flight and all. I wondered what their life span was, now that they'd been removed from their natural habitat.

I leaned into Spencer and stage-whispered, "I think my heels are cool." Cool, hot, tepid, lukewarm. Anything but fish food.

"If they're cool now, imagine how satiny-touchable they'll be after this one-of-a-kind treatment." She grasped my elbow, gentle but firm. "Mads," she said evenly, "Mother went to great lengths to arrange this for us and, therefore, is going to pitch a grade-A fit if we don't submit to the treatment. *With enthusiasm*. Besides, you can't tell me those Jimmy Choos you wore the other night didn't leave your feet covered in blisters."

"There might be some Band-Aid action going on underneath these slouchy boots," I admitted reluctantly. That's the thing about slouchy boots: They hide a lot. They're very forgiving, with the slouch and all.

"Awesome." She wrapped her delicate fingers around my wrist and dragged me toward the pedicure chairs.

Before I could say "wasabi," we were tilted back, side by side, our shoulder blades vibrating in tune with our massage chairs.

"Ahh," Spencer sighed, her throaty exhalation broken up into tinny, rhythmic beats. "This is more like it." She closed her eyes.

"This works," I conceded. If I didn't actually look down at my feet and into the water, I even found the whole fish-nibbling thing to be rather . . . tolerable. Enjoyable, even.

The truth was, some of the stuff that I'd done in my Choo-clad, very vino-ed state the other night had been pretty unforgivable. Meaning that I owe Spencer big-time. Even if she has no idea what happened—and *never will*—I decided that the least I could do was to suck it up and be cheerful about my newly appointed status as fish food.

I shifted my attention away from scaly little fish mouths and back over to my bestie. Other than that slightly weirdo e-mail exchange, we really hadn't had a deep heart-to-heart since the Hollywood Ball. Morning-after e-mails don't quite count anyway, what with fuzzy postcocktail brain and everything. And a lot of majorness had gone down at the ball—I wasn't the only girl getting her illicit flirt on. A blow-by-blow rehash of the night was *definitely* in order.

Um, with a few key details left out, of course.

"Okay. Spill," I said, tilting in my seat to face Spencer head-on.

"Hmm?" She opened her eyes, widening them in her best innocent expression. Like I didn't know better. Please—we practiced that look together on many a rainy Saturday back in the day. It's the reason our parents don't know about our early flirtations with imported Silk Cut ciggies (it didn't take).

"First off, you and Regan? Happily ever after?" The girlies had a history, after all. They'd been fast friends, and even faster enemies, though most of the badness had been concocted by Paige.

"There's definitely hope, after what went down the other night. So, you know, I think we're cool."

"And what about you and Jeremy? Why do I think there's a story there?"

I swear, the girl blushed to the tips of her ears. Bingo. Do I know Spencer, or what?

"There's no story." Her ears were going to burst into flame.

"A vignette, then? An interpretive dance? Perhaps a post-modern installation art display?"

Spencer shrugged. "Okay, I give. Maybe I've got a haiku for you."

Now it was my turn to wrinkle an eyebrow.

"Paint by numbers? Connect the dots?" Spencer wasn't giving up.

I scowled. "I'm not sure if you're fully aware of this, Spencer Grace," I said, using my best Mom-voice, "but I've traded in my pumice stone for a school of bloodthirsty guppies. For *you.* Now, I think that deserves a few of the gorier details, don't you?"

[Tavo break. Won't be a mo'.]

12/8, 9:38 p.m.
privacy setting: private collection

A CUT ABOVE (CONT.)

Mmm, calorie-free energy beverage! Also, Tyler just texted. He misses me. That was the whole text: *MISS U.*

Tyler misses me. It's nice to hear, even though we both know that what happened will *never* happen again. I'd feel guilty—I mean, I *do* feel guilty, but . . .

But what I mean to say is that I'd feel guilti*er,* if it weren't for the stuff Spencer copped to when we were getting our toes gnawed off by designer goldfish.

What she and Jeremy did, in the coatroom, while Tyler and I were . . . off on our own. How, when the coat check dude found them planting the stuff in Paige's stole, they completely sucked each other's faces off as part of a ruse.

A *ruse.* I'm so sure.

"Did it feel ruse-y?" I asked Spencer, concentrating fiercely on my toenails as Geoffroy's assistant lacquered them with bold, even streaks of OPI Catherine the Grape. I couldn't look her in the eye. I had too much at stake in her reply—and for all the wrong reasons.

It didn't matter. I could tell that she wasn't looking at me either.

"Um, not really," she said, so softly that I almost didn't hear her.

I wanted to grab her by the shoulders, to shout at her to speak up since she holds the key to my happiness in her perfect, French-manicured fingers. But I managed some self-restraint. My toenails were wet, after all. And I was already on Geoffroy's bad side. "But . . . ?" I prompted.

"But it was confusing," she said finally. "My feelings for Jeremy are always confusing."

"I know," I said. And I do know. Whatever Tyler and Spencer have now, Jer was definitely her first love. And if he hadn't gone off to Africa with his parents, who knows what would have happened between them?

Who knows what would have happened between Tyler and me?

"You've been confused for a while now," I said delicately, choosing my words as carefully as I could. "Like, ever since Jeremy came back from safari. Don't you think?"

She bit at her thumbnail, eliciting a *tsk* from Geoffroy, who was clearly way over us by now. She wedged her hands underneath her. "I know. But I'm not sure what to do about it."

Every cell in my body was urging me to encourage her to break up with Tyler and go for Jeremy. It's what she wants—I truly believe that. But ultimately, I decided to be more subtle.

"Maybe you should"—I winced—"follow your heart?" I don't love sounding like a Hallmark card, but sometimes the shortest distance between two points is a straight line.

She was silent. I was encouraged.

"Seriously," I went on. "If you felt something when you guys kissed, then Jeremy probably did too. Maybe you just need to go for it."

She bit her lip. "I don't know, Madison," she said. "I really have no idea. I almost wish I'd busted Paige on my own. Having Jeremy there only made things messier. It's like a thing that we're in on together. I don't . . ." She shook her head. "I don't know that I need to be *in* on something with Jeremy. Getting closer to him . . . it doesn't seem like a good idea when I'm still in love with Tyler."

Now it was my turn to stay silent.

She turned to me, her eyes bright and teary. No matter

what she'd decided to do, she was obviously totally frustrated and confused. My heart leaped. "Thanks, Madison," she said quietly.

"For what?" *For betraying you? For hooking up with your boyfriend? For stabbing you in the back? I'm sorry, Spence. I swear on my Miu Miu platform mary jane pumps, I never meant to do anything to hurt you.*

"For being such a good friend." She leaned over in her seat and kissed me quickly on the cheek. "Seriously. I don't know what I'd do without you."

location: the Closet
mood: guilt-ridden
ranking: Worst. Friend. Ever.

————————————

Ty_It_On: Hiya. Did u get my text?

Madison_Ave: Yup. Thx. ☺

Ty_It_On: But no reply?

Madison_Ave: I just sed, 'thx, happy face.' That's a reply!

Ty_It_On: So I heard u spent the day with Spencer.

Madison_Ave: U heard right.

Ty_It_On: U didn't say anything 2 her, did u?

Madison_Ave: R u insane? Never. No way. She'd never forgive us.

Madison_Ave: 2 be honest, I'm not sure that I forgive us. U know? I mean . . .

Ty_It_On: R u sorry that we hooked up? Cause I'm not. Madison, u know how I feel about you. This is lousy timing and everything, but it wasn't just a hookup to me.

Madison_Ave: Me neither.

Ty_It_On: And things have been a little messed up with Spencer since school started. U know, since Jeremy came back.

Madison_Ave: I know. But that doesn't change anything. Whatever is going on between us, we need 2 let it go. She's my best friend.

Ty_It_On: I get it. I love her 2.

Madison_Ave: Right. So it's agreed. We both love Spencer and don't want to see her get hurt. So whatever this is with us, it can't be anything anymore.

Ty_It_On: Right.

Madison_Ave: Right.

Ty_It_On: U said that already. ;)

Madison_Ave: I know. I'm hoping that if I repeat it enough, I'll get used to the idea.

Ty_It_On: How's that working out for you?

Madison_Ave: I'll let u know.

Ty_It_On: OK, I'm going to sign off. Rosie is calling us for dinner. I guess I'll see u in school?

Madison_Ave: C u then.

Ty_It_On: Mads?

Madison_Ave: ?

Ty_It_On: I do miss u, u know.

Madison_Ave: I know.

Madison_Ave: is doing the right thing. But that doesn't make it easy.

12/8, 11:28 p.m.
privacy setting: private collection

HOPE SPRINGS EPHEMERAL

Things that are easy for me:

    1. Applying pencil eyeliner

    2. Sight-reading music

    3. Making slice-and-bake cookies

Things that are less easy:

    1. Physics

    2. The rope climb in gym class

    3. Getting over my bestie's BF

I should probably be glad to hear that Tyler feels the same way about me as I do about him. That makes me a seminormal teenage girl as opposed to a backstabbing skank-whore with no sense of integrity. Like I told Spencer the other day, Tyler and I always *have* had a flirty relationship, and I *did* always think it was totally innocent. Always. It wasn't until we took that side trip to Smoochville that I realized that I've been digging on him for longer than I can remember. And the fact that he digs me too? Well, that makes him, if not perfect, at least not just some loser who steps out behind his girlfriend's back with whoever's available.

Besides, he said they've been distant lately, right? And I should know better than anyone that Spencer's been feeling it too. The truth is, Spencer is kind of the *cause* of the distance between them, since she's still all kinds of conflicted about Jeremy.

So, maybe, could there be a chance that this will all work itself out? That we'll all get our happily-ever-afters after all? Spencer will break it off with Tyler and go for Jeremy, who seems to be the one she truly wants. And then Tyler and I will be free to get together for real.

In this scenario, everyone's a winner.

There's a chance that it could all go down that way, that things could all fall into place. I just need to do the right thing, to do right by Spencer. If her relationship with Tyler is unraveling, then I can be there for her while the threads unspool. Once she's pulled herself back together (with the help of the most supportive friend ever), she'll realize that moving on from Tyler is the best thing that could ever happen to her.

How does the saying go? "Good things come to those who wait." Here's hoping there's some truth to the old adage. Waiting may not be easy, but in this case, it's worth it.

Here's to happy endings for all of us.

location: bed
status: lady-in-waiting
hoping: against hope

12/10, 8:52 a.m., by Kaylen Turner

A CLEAN BREAK

FYI, for any of you Bradfordians who've been dying for the 411 on Paige Andrews, I've got the scoop—and it's straight from the pretty pony's mouth.

Apparently, life on the inside isn't half bad. I mean, rehab on a private island in Turks and Caicos isn't exactly Alcatraz. So, yeah, they're up at the crack of dawn—but, hey, so are those of us who haven't had the dumb luck of being born with naturally pin-straight hair, right? First there's meditation and Bikram yoga—you know, the really, really hot kind where you get all sweaty and limp and kind of want to die—led by the world-famous guru Swami Vivasingh. Anyway, she says it clears her mind and is all therapeutic and stuff.

And then breakfast. (Strictly gourmet. The restaurant's five-star.)

They do group therapy and support circles in the mornings. (It's über-confidential, but I will just say that a certain former E! Entertainment *Wild On* starlet shares the talking stick with Paige. And I heard that Bravo is considering maybe filming a new reality show based on Paige and her experience in rehab. So there's kind of a lot going on there, in group.)

And then the patients have free time to participate in recuperation and recreation therapies. Deep-tissue massage, skin detoxification treatments, body wrapping, paddle boarding . . . I swear, that girl is all about the self-improvement. It's inspiring.

Paige says that her shrink thinks she's on the verge of a real breakthrough, and Paige has even been saying that she *might* have taken some people at Bradford for granted, but she isn't going to anymore. (If you have to ask, it's definitely not you.)

So that's the story.

Cell phone use is limited and her e-mail is monitored, so if you have a message, card, gift, or whatever that you want to pass along to Paige, you can send it through me, and I'll make sure that she gets it.

2 RESPONSES TO "A CLEAN BREAK"

Miss_Stick says: Give it up, Kaylen. Paige's bust is totally old news. Just like Paige.

Cap'nCrunch says: I heard the only thing limited about Paige's cell phone is the incoming call log. No wonder she's so chatty with you, QweenKayleen.

12/10, 12:11 p.m.
privacy setting: ready-to-wear

EVERYTHING OLD IS FIERCE AGAIN

I have news of the mostest variety:

Aggie over at Destroyed Girl called this morning and told me that she "totally and absolutely hearted" (direct quote, her words, not mine) the repurposed bag samples that I showed her last month (her fave was the hobo with the Hermès handle). She met with her buyer, and they're going to stock a quantity of Glamourista originals! She wants my spring collection. All of it!

Squee!

So, okay, the fabbity news is that she wants stock as early in the new year as possible. Which is also kind of the stressy news, seeing as how New Year's is, like, FIVE MINUTES FROM NOW. And my spring collection currently consists of three pieces.

I mean, they're three *kick-ass* pieces, but still.

I'll need more. ASAP.

I can do it. I don't care. I'll mainline caffeine, Red Bull, diet pills—whatever it takes. (Come to think of it, it's kind of a shame Paige isn't around. She'd probably be able to get her hands on some primo Adderall.)

(*Kidding.* Sort of.)

There are sketches to pencil, vintage fabrics to track down, samples to have stitched. Frankly, I don't even have time to finish this blog. More later.

And did I mention—*squee*?

!!

location: the Bradbrary
status: squee to the third power
stress levels: high. Like, neon high.

COMMENTS (6):

GoldenGirl says: That is the veriest of pieces of news! And I have more: Mother wants you to show your collection at the Runway for Hope charity fashion show in February. How phenom is that? This is why you are our glamourista! XOXO

CaliforniaChic says: What she said. This calls for a celebration! Dinner? Tonight? Soirée? Saketini?

Madison_Ave says: You guys rule. I wish I could do dinner, but I'm way too excited to eat and I think I'm going to be locked in the Closet from now until D-day (delivery day). It's that whole good news/bad news thing.

GoldenGirl says: She's right, though. We need to do something. How about an after-school shopping trip? You can write it off as inspiration.

Madison_Ave says: What an *inspired* suggestion. Okay, twist my arm. I'm in! Meet you guys in the lounge after last period.

CaliforniaChic says: We're there!

12/10, 10:11 p.m.
privacy setting: private collection

WHOLESALE GIRL BONDAGE

Via a little retail therapy, as per usual.

Walnut Street in Center City is pretty much the upscale shopping center of the world. The ABCs of Rittenhouse Row? More like the Armani Exchange, Bebe, Club Monaco, etc. I could happily spend the day there shopping my way through the alphabet. And today I almost did. With a little help from my friends.

It wasn't just about the massive thrill of wanton consumption either (though that's always good times). I mean, Spencer, Regan, and I are just starting to settle into a dynamic together. A Paige-less dynamic, that is. Things are way different now, with her off drying out. Less drama, for starters, and a wee bit less psychopathic emotional instability.

There's really no arguing that toward the end there, Paige was rapidly deteriorating into a bad Lifetime movie of the week. Now, without her, we're bright and shiny, new and improved. We're *it.* And as of this afternoon we've got the bright and shiny shopping bags to prove it. We're rapidly becoming a threesome, an unholy trinity. And I don't think that's going to change anytime soon—no matter how many times a day Kaylen texts us to see what we're up to.

"She needs to chillax," I said, glancing at Kaylen's most recent missive on my iPhone, rolling my eyes and pausing to admire a pair of crisp white boot-cut jeans in the window of Diesel. "I totally need a pair of white jeans for Palm Beach."

"You do need a pair of white jeans for Palm Beach," Regan agreed, not the least bit concerned that we have no concrete plans to go to Palm Beach in the immediate future. Love that girl. She yanked the door to the shop open and led the three of us inside. "And also a pair of yellow skinnies."

"Have those," I responded. "I've been saving them for Aspen."

Unlike Palm Beach, Aspen is already majorly in the works. New Year's blowout. None of us can wait.

That's a thing about me: I get way excited about trips and planning special outfits for special places, which means that there's a lot in my closet at any given time that's been earmarked for an event or occasion that's practically light-years away. I like to think that's part of my charm. It's good to have extra pieces around, anyway; I never know what's going to end up going into a day's look.

So, yeah: yellow skinnies. With a black knit Theory cashmere sweater. A little conservative for me . . . until you see the shoes I've set aside to go with.

"Is that Kaylen *again*?" Spencer clucked, as this time Regan's phone buzzed. Regan hit Ignore and rolled her eyes. "It's getting to be a little sad."

"*Getting* to be?" I raised an eyebrow. I mean, Kaylen is nice enough . . .

Actually, you know what? That's not even true. Kaylen is kind of a clingy bitch. And, like I said, it's *always* been a little sad. Even though she does have really pretty hair.

"I thought she was busy actively being all in touch with Paige, not that Zephyr really allows that," Regan said, fingering a pair of black jeans with rhinestone trim at the pockets. "Eighties retro good or eighties retro bad?"

I gave the pants a closer examination, pursing my lips. "We could do a better job with a BeDazzler at home. If you don't mind sacrificing your Chip and Peppers to a worthy cause." I knew she wouldn't.

25

She grinned, white and wide. "That's why you're our Mads."

We had made it all the way through to the Js of our impromptu alphabetical splurge when I saw it—just a flash of metal out of the corner of my well-practiced eye (I am nothing if not a seasoned shopper). It was in the window of Jack Kellmer Jewelers, a store I don't generally go into unless I'm picking up a birthday gift for my father, but this thing called out to me like a siren at sea.

A sterling silver flask.

I know, I know, flasks can be a little tacky; substance abuse chic is *so* last season. But I was one thousand and fifty-two percent certain that it was the most perfect Christmas gift ever.

For Tyler.

Tyler's a party animal, and a guy of extremely discerning taste. This was a gift that would fit him like a glove, make him feel like a high roller. Or like *more* of a high roller, assuming that was even possible. It would help him realize his inner dream of becoming a living, breathing extra from the movie *Swingers*, which, while not something he'd ever explicitly stated as a secret desire, I knew was the private image that he had of himself. The surface of the flask was smooth, and I knew it'd be easy enough to have it monogrammed. To make it even more personal, unique.

I reached out, almost as though I could put my hand through the glass and take the flask with me. As though it would be that easy, and Spencer would never have to know that I was buying any sort of token for her boyfriend. That I was in a position to be giving her boyfriend semi-intimate gifts. That I'd ever been in *any* sort of position with her boyfriend at all.

From over my shoulder, I heard Spencer gasp.

My heart sank. Not only would I not be able to give the flask—

or *any* Christmas gift, for that matter—to Tyler, but of course, Spencer would want it for herself. Now that she'd seen it, she'd buy it, have it engraved with Tyler's initials, have it professionally wrapped with thick, creamy paper and real sprigs of holly and maybe even mistletoe. *She'd* be the one to give it to Tyler.

She is Tyler's girlfriend.

"Ohmigod." She was actually drooling in my ear. My heart was broken, torn, shredded—and my shoulder was getting soggy. Awesomeness.

"Those *earrings*," Regan breathed, reaching her fingers out in the same hypnotic state with which I'd first approached the flask. But she wasn't reaching in the direction of the flask, and come to think of it, neither was Spencer. I followed their zombie gazes. "I think those are Majorca black pearls."

"Set in rose gold," Spencer confirmed. "Want. Need. Must have." She marched forward, brandishing her signature Hermès Kelly bag like a weapon. Which, in a way, I guess, it was. She was Diana, Goddess of the Hunt.

It wasn't the flask she was after. I couldn't decide if that made things better or worse.

It didn't matter, of course. Either way, Tyler was still her boyfriend.

We made our way inside, and Regan and Spencer rushed to the counter to try on the earrings. I followed halfheartedly behind them but soon found myself aggressively contemplating a platinum cuff bracelet that just *happened* to be housed in the same case as the flask.

It was a really nice bracelet. Even if I did already have one just like it. In rose gold, no less.

I was so preoccupied that I didn't hear Spencer and Regan until they were on top of me again, flanking me as they gabbed about I had no idea what.

"You didn't like them?" I managed to choke out. Spencer

was earringless, carrying only the three or four shopping bags she'd had when we first went into the shop, which shocked me. Spencer is a sucker for rose gold. Girl has taste.

Spencer shrugged. "They were totally gorj. But if I don't buy them now, then I know what Tyler's going to get me for Christmas." She giggled. "Too bad I have no idea what I'm going to get for him."

Too bad.

She linked her elbow through my own, still laughing. "Regan wants gelato despite the subzero temp. Shall we indulge her temporary insanity? Capogiro?"

She didn't give me a chance to reply.

location: the Closet
status: heart: still broken, torn, shredded. Shoulder: currently dry.
sound track: the Rolling Stones. Oldies but goodies. 'Cause
you really *can't* always get what you want. Sob.

12/11, 10:59 a.m., by Spencer Kelly

THE BIG CHILL

Here's your reminder that the Sisters of the Main Line Annual Winter Cocktail Party is upon us. And while I know that cocktails are their own means to an end, I'd also like to give you the heads-up that our own glamourista and virtuoso cellist, Madison Takahashi, will be giving one of her muchly demanded solo performances.

Come chill with us, Bradfordians. Maybe if you're lucky, Mads will dedicate a number to you.

Eh, probably not. But, you know, here's hoping!

Besos,

Spencer

3 RESPONSES TO "THE BIG CHILL"

CaliforniaChic says: How cool. I'm in, of course.

QweenKayleen says: Totes! I'm so there.

MasterCeej says: Can't wait to chill with a hottie like Mads! Rad.

GoldenGirl: Let's go out on the town tonight so Mads can blow off some steam before the big performance tomorrow.

GoldenGirl: I'm thinking Lucky Strike Lanes for a change of pace?

CaliforniaChic: How swank! Sounds good to me!

Madison_Ave: I think I have the perfect outfit—I'll see you there!

12/13, 1:33 a.m.
privacy setting: private collection

BOWL ME OVER

I am sorry to say that Lucky Strike Lanes did not live up to the high promise of its extremely suggestive moniker.

Retro-hip bowling may *sound* like a good idea—and, in fact, it did, when Spencer suggested it—but I wouldn't go so far as to say that our evening there brought any of us luck.

I mean, okay, fine, if we're going to get all technical about it, then yes, I did get somewhat lucky at various points over the course of the night (nothing south of the border—it was a *bowling alley,* after all). But that's neither here nor there. And also, not necessarily lucky, depending on how you're looking at things.

The point is, the night was messiness. And ugliness. And people striking out all over the place. Am I mixing my sports metaphors? What can I say? Bowling was never really my game. And after tonight it's probably never, ever going to be either.

Yesterday Spencer decided we needed to party, and while most of us would have been happy to hit Saketini for the standard Takahashi VIP treatment courtesy of my dear old dad, she thought Lucky Strike would be a kitschy (but still swank) good time. The competitive beast in Spencer then decided to raise the stakes by assembling a crowd, hence the invites extended to C.J., Dalton, Tyler, Kaylen, and even Jeremy (via Regan). More proof that the post-Paige tide is ever-turning. I can't imagine that Jeremy and Paige would have willingly spent a Friday night together back in the good old days.

We girlies met at Spencer's place to do some quick lemon-drop shots in the carriage house and admire one another looking our veriest, after which point we dashed off to Lucky Strike to join the rest of the crew.

"This place is wild," Regan said when we arrived, straining to be heard above the booming drum-and-bass rhythm that practically had the walls bouncing in and out to the beat. Her eyes flickered across the cavernous room, taking in the excessive neon lighting, the go-go-costumed waitresses, and the impossibly slinky, well-heeled clientele. "Are those people even here to bowl?" She pointed at a pair of girls so skinny, they could have been Nicole Richie's anorexic sisters. Their legs bowed, ankles straining against lethal stilettos.

I shrugged. I doubted they'd even be able to pick up a bowling ball. From the languid poses they'd struck against the bar, my guess was they were waiting to be noticed by some members of the male persuasion. I decided I didn't care about the skinny bizzniches. I was too busy drinking in the Lucky Strike vibes. It was like being trapped inside a giant jukebox. I was digging it. The air smelled of appletinis and possibility.

"Where is everyone?" Regan asked. She spoke with exaggeration so that we could read her lips. Smart girl.

Spencer glanced at her phone. "They're at lane twenty-one. But first"—her eyes twinkled wickedly—"you're going to see something phenomenal." Spencer clapped her hands together. "Madison Takahashi—in *bowling shoes*!"

Now it was my turn to frown. "Nothing phenomenal about that. I mean, whatever. I can slum it with the best of them," I protested, pouting.

"Right," Spencer said, clearly not buying it. "That's why you're wearing Lacoste." She pointed one smoothly polished fingernail directly at my torso.

"It's a T-shirt dress," I insisted, giving myself a quick once-over.

She had a point, though. It was an *expensive* T-shirt dress. My torso was designer-clad. The dress was vintage, though I'd altered the hem and the collar and added a belt of my own design. I'd had to scour three separate consignment shops to find it. *And* another four for the scarf I'd twisted into a contrasting headband.

So maybe slumming's not my thing. Whatever. At least bowling shoes are comfy, even if it is a little gross to absorb countless other people's accumulated foot sweat.

I decided not to think too much about it.

"Let's go," I said, taking charge and marching toward the shoe rental counter.

Ah, yes. Bowling shoes. As predicted, mine looked spectacular with my dress. One would almost think that I'd planned it that way. Hee. But I wasn't giggling for long. We made our way over to lane twenty-one and found Kaylen, C.J., Dalton, and Tyler well into their first rounds—of bowling, as well as booze. That much was obvious from the slanted grin that Kaylen gave us as we approached. When she stood, I realized that there was one more player behind her. And he was most definitely *not* smiling.

Jeremy.

Regan had worked hard to convince him to meet up with us, but the shots in the carriage house had put us a bit behind schedule. I wondered just how long he'd been here waiting for us. I mean, he's not exactly known for palling around with those guys. One glance at his stony expression told me: too long.

"Damage control," Regan sang under her breath, tiptoeing delicately forward and sidling up next to Jer on the couch. Spencer strolled forward and kissed Tyler hello while I pointedly hugged Kaylen (I may have been overcompensating) and kissed C.J. on the cheek. Out of the corner of my eye, I could see Tyler and Spencer's kiss taking a turn for the PG-13. I grabbed Kaylen's wrist.

"What are you drinking?" I yelled.

She brandished a muddy-looking cocktail. "Chocotinis!" She swigged at her drink. "Yum!"

I flagged down a waitress, posthaste.

Muddy looking or no, chocotinis are actually quite delicious. And during the course of imbibing drinks one through three, I was starting to feel relaxed and happy about life. I had my besties, we were cruising toward the holidays, and I didn't even mind that Tyler's arm seemed to be Velcro-ed to Spencer's hip.

Okay, well, maybe I minded a little bit. But not *that* much.

Did I mention the part about how Spencer's crazy competitive? It comes in handy in certain aspects of her life, like with grades and schoolwork, or in field hockey and stuff. And in theory, it could have been an asset to our bowling field trip. In *theory*. Alas, her brilliantissimo idea of playing a battle of the sexes round backfired. Rather brilliantissimo-ly.

By this point in the evening, I wasn't the only one who'd gotten extremely friendly with the happy juice, and a certain amount of good-natured ribbing was beginning to rear its head.

"Suck it!" Regan shrieked, doing a full-on *Saturday Night Fever* dance from the lane to her seat as her sparkly pink bowling ball crashed against the pins in spectacular strikeage. This was her third in a row. (Maybe bowling skills are a West Coast thing? Maybe she's a hustler? A ringer? Inquiring minds WANT TO KNOW.)

Despite his gender alliances, Jeremy leaped up and high-fived her, grabbing at her hand and grinning warmly.

Watching Jeremy and Regan, I realized . . . well, that I wasn't the only one watching Jeremy and Regan. Spencer had witnessed their secret handshake as well—and the look on her face suggested she was taking it about as well as I'd taken her smoochfest with Tyler earlier on.

Jeremy picked up his ball (a more understated dark purple number) and made his way to the lane. At the same time a small smile crept across Spencer's lips, telling me that she was most definitely up to something. Jeremy reached back, looking for all the world like the tiny metal dude at the top of a bowling trophy (which is to say, way professional and all that), which suggested to me that he was going to kick those pins' collective asses, and just as he released—

"GUTTER BALL!" Spence grabbed his shoulders to surprise him and shouted directly into his ear.

Jeremy jumped about thirteen feet into the air and dropped the ball. It thudded loudly and began to wobble weakly toward the gutter. He whirled around to find Spencer doubled over laughing.

"Cheater." His eyes widened with incredulity. "You. Are a cheater." He tilted his head at her, mock disappointment radiating from his pores.

"It's not my fault if you're easily distracted." Spencer giggled and leaned into him with a playful nudge.

Beside me, Tyler stiffened, his body going as rigid as the plastic seats. His disappointment was not of the mock variety, that much was clear.

Awkward much?

The whole thing was starting to play like a telenovela: Spencer stalking Jeremy, Tyler stalking Spencer, and me stalking Tyler. If only Regan, C.J., and Kaylen would run off to have a threesome in the bathroom, we'd be all set.

I suddenly wanted to barf.

Desperate for some head-clearing and thought-collecting, I made my way to the bathroom and splashed some cold water on my cheeks, taking care not to mess with my nonwaterproof Lancôme Definicils mascara. I blinked at my reflection in the mirror. Mirror Mads was hanging in, but barely. Her forehead was a touch shiny, which was easily addressed with some blotting paper, and her eyes were red, which needed nothing more than a few drops of Visine. But other than that, I guessed that maybe she looked ready to roll. Or should I say, ready to bowl? Ha.

I took a deep breath, ran my fingers through the small section of electric blue tips dyed in my hair, and stepped back out into the dark hallway. Only to find that Tyler was waiting for me.

"What . . . ?"

I let myself trail off. The truth was, I didn't really *want* to know "what." Nothing good could come of any of this, but that didn't change the fact that all I wanted, in this moment, was to be kissing Tyler. So, instead of talking, I stepped forward, desire seeping from every cell of my body.

He understood what I needed. And he obliged.

His mouth was soft against mine, then harder, more urgent. He buried his fingers in my hair. I wanted to melt, thought I might actually *be* melting. I couldn't tell where my body ended and his began, and I didn't much want to, either. Except . . .

"Wait." I forced myself to press away from him, to look him in the eye. A brown curl dangled across his forehead, and I willed myself not to brush it back. "We can't."

He bit his lip. Nodded. "It's just . . . I can't help it. I miss you. I *want* you." His words sliced through me, like a handful of ice cubes dropped into the pit of my stomach.

"We promised we weren't going to do this anymore. Because of Spencer."

"This isn't about Spencer."

I leveled him with a look. "Really?" I had to call him out. I had to know—even if knowing was painful. "This has nothing to do with how flirty she was being with Jeremy back there? You're not kissing me to get even with her?"

Tyler's eyes flashed. I *love* his eyes when they get all flashy. "Don't you give me more credit than that? I don't care about her and Jeremy. Even if she does have some kind of history with that loser, she's with *me* now. But that's not the point."

"It's not?" I hated to admit it, but it was sounding kind of pointy to me.

Tyler took my hand in his. "I know what we promised. I know how this looks. But you've got to believe me. Now that . . . well, you know—now that we've been together, I can't go back to the way things were. I need you, Madison."

I didn't know what to say to that.

"There you are!" Now it was my turn to jump thirteen feet in the air, my hand snapping back into its normal place by my side.

"Mads, you're up," Spencer said. She reached out and smoothed Tyler's hair like I'd wanted to. He didn't flinch or pull away. They moved naturally together, comfortable with each other's bodies, each other's physical presence. Not worried that someone was watching. "We were looking for you."

"Yeah, I found Madison when I came out of the bathroom," Tyler said, quickly composing himself. "She wasn't feeling so good. I was going to take her to the bar to get her some club soda or something."

At least it explained the nauseated look that I knew was plastered across my face. Give the boy credit for a rockin' cover story.

"Yeah, okay. You two do that. I'm going to go back to the game. But"—Spencer leaned in close now, her face plaintive—"I think something weird is going on."

"What? Who? Weird? No." *Shut up, Madison.*

"No, seriously." Her eyes were round. "Dalton and Regan. There's some serious bicker-banter going on between them."

I wanted to faint, I was so relieved. But still—"Huh," I said. "Well, you know, bicker-banter doesn't really mean that much. Call me if it begins to morph into banter-flirt." But I doubted that would happen. Dalton is really not Regan's type. Insofar as I know what Regan's type is, never having known her to date anyone other than Ryder Jared, and only having witnessed that relationship through the tabloids.

Spencer shrugged. "I'm just calling it like I see it. Just because they haven't realized it yet doesn't mean there isn't chemistry."

I wasn't convinced, but at least Spencer's preoccupation with Dalton and Regan meant that for now, the heat was off of me. I decided to go with it.

"I wonder what Jeremy thinks about their connection," Spencer added as an afterthought. "Or if he and Regan truly are platonic buddies."

"Whatever," Tyler said. "I'm gonna go get that club soda." He stalked off.

Spencer sighed. "He has *serious* issues with Jeremy."

"Um, yeah." I dropped my gaze. "Right." And then I went quiet again. Luckily, Spencer was too preoccupied to notice.

location: the family room
status: woolly-headed, cotton-mouthed
filmography: my favorite hangover flick: *Clueless.* Brainless fashion, sharp satire, cute boys. It's the holy trifecta. I can recite it by heart.

to: GoldenGirl@bradfordprep.com,
Madison_Ave@bradfordprep.com,
CaliforniaChic@bradfordprep.com
from: QweenKayleen@bradfordprep.com
date: 12/13, 11:43 a.m.
re: Carpooling

Hey, girlfriends—

Anyone up for sharing a ride to the Sisters of the Main
Line winter bash tonight? Daddy rented me a *fierce* stretch
Hummer, and there's plenty of room for friends (and dates, of
course).

Should be very. I can't wait! And, Mads—good luck with the
performance and stuff.

Smooches,

K

to: QweenKayleen@bradfordprep.com
from: GoldenGirl@bradfordprep.com
date: 12/13, 11:47 a.m.
re: Carpooling

Hey, Kaylen:

Thanks so muchly for the invite, but Tyler's driver is taking us in his father's classic Jag. I think he wants some private time, you know? (Boys! So needy!)

Anyway, we'll see you there.

Besos.

xx,

Spencer

to: QweenKayleen@bradfordprep.com
from: Madison_Ave@bradfordprep.com
date: 12/13, 11:49 a.m.
re: Carpooling

Hi, Kaylen—

Ooh, wish I could, but I have to get there all early and
whatever to set up for the performance.

(I know, I'm a diva.)

Thanks for the good-luck wishes!

Mwah!

Madison

_____

to: QweenKayleen@bradfordprep.com
from: CaliforniaChic@bradfordprep.com
date: 12/13, 11:53 a.m.
re: Carpooling

Kaylen!

You are the sweetest! Alas, I've already sworn to Jer that I'd
ride with him (payback for dragging him to Lucky Strike last
night). And you know he's not really a Hummer kind of guy.

Save us a seat at the recital if you get there first!

Later,

Reegs

12/14, 1:08 p.m., by Kaylen Turner

NOTEWORTHY GOINGS-DOWN

Hola, Bradfordians:

QweenKayleen here with the lowdown on last night's Sisters of the Main Line Annual Winter Cocktail Party. Unfortunately, there were no chocotinis in sight, those Sisters preferring to kick it old school and stuff. Strictly a G&T crowd, plus the requisite Veuve Clicquot Rosé, natch. *Slurp, slurp, yum.*

Madison Takahashi warmed up the crowd by sending chills down their spines with some totally mad cello skills, and her dad kept us stuffed and satisfied with Kobe tartar pinwheels, blowfish sashimi, and rock shrimp tempura. I repeat: *yum.* No wonder Food Network is courting him so heavily. He just gets better and better.

But *anyway*, the hottest news of the evening had nothing to do with dining, décor, or even a performance from an up-and-coming young diva (and of course I use the term in the strictest sense; Madison is poised for stardom, not that *that* is any kind of news).

In fact, *some* people didn't seem interested in any of that at all.

Oh, fine. Coy has never really been my thing. I'll just say it: Regan Stanford and Dalton Richmond.

Yes, that's right. They may have arrived separately, but they sat together—*extremely* together—during the performance, and let me tell you, they were fifty different kinds of chatty and stuff. She clearly doesn't know that Mr. FilthyRich is hardly uncharted territory.

I'm sorry, but really, it's true: It looks like someone is scoping out Paige Andrews's sloppy seconds during her unfortunate absence. Ewness.

Come on, Regan. You're on the Main Line now. You're too good for hand-me-downs. Or, you know, so I hope. For your sake and stuff.

2 RESPONSES TO "NOTEWORTHY GOINGS-DOWN"

FilthyRich says: Try minding your own f'ing business once in a while, K. Or soon *you'll* be the one going down.

CaliforniaChic says: Seriously, Kaylen. If you're going to dish, at least get your story straight. Does the fact that I had Spencer on my other side mean I'm suddenly swinging both ways too? Please—I was far too busy listening to Mads's amazing performance to be chatting up anyone (of either persuasion).

12/14, 1:29 p.m.
privacy setting: ready-to-wear

À LA CLOSET DINING

Seriously, girls. It's the next best thing to al fresco or à la carte. That is, if your closet is anything like mine—six hundred square feet, lined with built-ins, lit to specification, and furnished with an expansive architectural desk for sketching. Maybe I'm just (re)stating the obvious, but I *heart* my closet. It only makes sense that eating in here would be one more stiletto-heeled step toward attaining my own personal Nirvana.

Oh, who am I kidding? Yeah, I love my closet. But burnt toast for Sunday brunch is a major bummer. Even if I'm eating it surrounded by my favorite designer samples. Jimmy Choo can only do so much for me in my hour of need.

As you know, Sunday brunch is normally Master Chef Takahashi's territory; our cook gets the morning off, and Dad whirls around the kitchen like a Tasmanian devil, tossing anything he can get his hands on into blenders, poachers, pressure cookers, and juicers, testing recipes for his empire, but more importantly, providing a feast for his much loved fam. It's our tradition. It's the one constant on the roller coaster that is his sensationally successful professional existence.

Or, at least, it *was*.

I woke this morning on the earlier side (that is to say, it was still in the a.m., which, for a Sunday, is not to be scoffed at), feeling rested and not a little bit self-satisfied. My recital last night went well; even I can admit that, and I finally nailed that passage in the Kodály Cello Sonata op. 8 that was giving me so much trouble. The Sisters, a veritable true-life Prada mafia, seemed pleased. My buds were in attendance (and, Reegs, I'm not even going to comment on Kaylen's blog post, here or otherwise—sheesh), and the rosé champagne was flowing. All was well in the world. And now, the morning after, it was time for me to slide down to the kitchen and hang out with my dad.

I slipped my cashmere robe on over my pj's, knotted my hair into a messy twist on top of my head, and wandered out of my bedroom and toward the kitchen.

It didn't take long to notice that something was up this fine morning. The room was dark, but more than that, there was a complete and utter absence of delicious and hunger-causing smells wafting in my direction. Not even the gentle, reassuring hum of the espresso machine.

Not good.

I found Mom seated at the breakfast bar, tapping her fingers against the marble-topped island, peering into an empty cup of coffee. Which was *extra* weird, since Mom usually has an IV drip of caffeine going on between the hours of nine a.m. and twelve p.m.

She looked up at me sleepily, as though surprised to discover me there. Curiouser and curiouser.

"Good morning, Madison," she said at last, her voice still fuzzy with sleep. "Do you want some . . . ?" she trailed off, noticing at last that her cup was actually empty. "I guess I should make some coffee."

"I'll do it," I said hastily. Let's not forget the Great Sanka

Fiasco, when Mom was caught making instant coffee when she thought Dad was out playing golf. Barf. She is not to be trusted with the hot beverages. "Where's Dad?" I allowed myself the fleeting hope that he'd made a quick run to the Ardmore Farmer's Market for some prosciutto or fresh fruit, but a leaden tug at the base of my stomach suggested otherwise.

Mom sighed, and I felt that blossom of hope deflate. "He had to go to New York, sweetie," she said. I thought I detected a hint of impatience at the edge of her voice, but it was gone before I could say for sure. "That Food Network special, don't you remember? They're filming this morning."

I did not, in fact, remember. Mainly because no one had bothered to tell me. Mainly because no one ever tells me anything.

Taking my silence for confusion, Mom forged ahead. "He's been wildly successful in Philly since his comeback, of course, but his brand is on the verge of exploding nationally again. He needs to work triple-time if he wants to take advantage of all of the opportunities opening up for him right now."

Great, so now I was getting the *E! True Hollywood Story* of my father's life. When all I'd really wanted was my Sunday-morning eggs Florentine.

"You can still have your eggs," Mom said, in a freaky moment of mother mind reading. "I can make them for you."

"Um, that's okay," I said quickly. The only event more memorable than the Sanka Fiasco is the Omelet Incident. The mere thought of that morning makes my throat close up in protest. "I'm not that hungry anyway." No, those roaring sounds coming from inside my stomach were just a chorus of tiny elves doing a dance of happiness for my father's continued success.

"I'll make some toast and head back to my room. I have some sketching to do." I *do* have to work on my spring collection, after all. Dad isn't the only one in the family poised for a major breakout.

I don't know who I thought I was fooling. Maybe Mom was just brain-dead enough to buy my story, but I've been in the Closet for almost an hour now, and the only thing I have to show for my designing efforts is a large white square of paper covered in a light dusting of toast crumbs. I'm just not feeling inspired this morning.

This is hopeless. Forget it. I've got a better idea:
When the going gets tough, the tough go shopping.
Who's in?

location: the Closet
status: irked—and also, still hungry
solution: consumer affairs?

COMMENTS (3):

GoldenGirl says: Oh, Maddie! I'm sorry your dad's so busy. I wish I could come over there and make you my famous scrambled eggs in consolation, but I have an appointment here with Hans to get my lowlights retouched. And you know how impossible it is to get an appointment with him. Maybe we can hang tonight?

CaliforniaChic says: Me too, on the later-ness. I promised Jeremy I'd go to that Rick Moody reading at the Free Library this afternoon. But that won't take all day. Let's check in later and come up with some kind of plan.

Madison_Ave says: Hmmph. I see how it is. Well, fine, then. I'm off.

12/14, 3:45 p.m.
privacy setting: private collection

HOLY GABBANA!

OMG. OMG. OMG.

I can't believe I did that.

!!!

I may be having a low-grade panic attack. Either that, or the stomach elves are on protest.

I guess it's a good thing the friendlies decided to opt out of this shopping spree.

O.

M.

G.

location: Starbucks—the cleanest getaway I could find
status: freaked out
crimes committed: well, the one, technically. But it was kind of victimless. Um, sort of.

12/14, 4:22 p.m.
privacy setting: private collection

POSTCARDS FROM THE EDGE

Taking deep breaths now.

Feeling slightly better. The stomach elves, at least, have ceased their panicked parade.

One decaf Tazo chai later, and some meditation to the tunes of the latest 'Bucks coffeehouse mix, and I think I'm ready to talk about what just went down.

What just happened sort of just . . . *happened.* Like, one minute I was standing in Jasmine, admiring a pair of Chanel aviators. And then, all of a sudden, it was like there was this whooshing sound that just filled my ears—like static or white noise, but powerful, radiating throughout my entire body. My fingertips twitched, and then, almost against my will, I grabbed at the glasses and dropped them down my sleeve.

I don't know why.

I hadn't planned to take them. I sure don't need them—I already have those limited-edition Wayfarers that I picked up that weekend in AC that I haven't taken out of the box yet—and it wasn't like I couldn't have just paid for them anyway. But something *happened.* Like my brain just went into autopilot and my body wasn't even my own.

Feeling the plastic frames cool against the inside of my arm, I hazarded a glance around the store. An emaciated-looking brunette salesclerk was holding a mirror up to a Juicy-clad soccer mom clearly taking a day off. I contemplated warning her against the purple Betsey Johnson frames she was trying on, then realized that this was not the best time for that sort of intervention.

I took a deep, introspective breath. And then I bolted. I *bolted.* Like some kind of Clyde-less Bonnie, or cat burglar, or freak-show klepto. Totally.

I really don't know what came over me. I guess I was just still pissed about Dad and the whole brunch thing. I mean, it's not like this is the first time his quest for world domination has interfered with family bonding. He was busy at the cocktail party the other night and missed the opening bars of my solo, which was not exactly his coolest, most Dad-of-the-Year moment, and when I tried to talk to him about my stress over the order from Destroyed Girl, he interrupted our heart-to-heart to take a business call. It's not like we've been all with the warm-and-fuzzy of late. So I guess there's that.

It wasn't always like this. Sunday brunches aside, once upon a time, I was his sous-chef. We experimented with crazy recipes before every family holiday, occasionally erupting into a boisterous food fight like some cheesy *People* magazine spread. I *like* cheesy magazine-spread food fights.

And it's starting to look like the only ones taking place in our foreseeable future will have to actually be scheduled by *People, Martha Stewart Living, Gourmet,* and the like. And handled by my dad's media managers. Good luck pinning him down, folks. He's always on the road these days.

Whatever. Poor me. I've joined Paige in the Lifetime movie cliché hall of fame, it's true. Daddy doesn't love me, so I've turned to a life of crime. *Waahh waahh waahh.*

And though I didn't step into Jasmine planning to take anything, of course, the truth is that I *liked* the shoplifting. It was thrilling. That fuzzy white noise that buzzed in my head actually managed, for a moment, to drown out the drama of my dad's elsewhereness, the pressure of designing my collection, the angst over me hooking up with Tyler, and the ugly, black feeling that coats the inside of my throat whenever I have to lie to Spencer about what happened between her boyfriend and her best friend. For just a moment it all went away. I was living in, and for, that moment.

Disturbing, no?

And what really scares me is that a moment is not nearly enough. I want more of that buzz. I want to do it again. That white noise that drowned out everything else is humming quietly, temporarily tamped down but certainly not gone for good. It's going to come back, louder, stronger. And then what?

I just really don't know.

location: still Starbucks. They sure do love their John Mayer here, huh?
status: slightly calmer
fingers: still a tad sticky

QweenKayleen: is hoping to be "committeed"!

 THE BRADFORD BLOG

12/16, 3:01 p.m., by Spencer Kelly

THE NEW SOCIAL ORDER

I've heard some rumors around the halls over the past few days, and I wanted to set the record straight.

I am thrilled to announce that the social committee has chosen a new executive board member. In the wake of Paige Andrews's sudden and unforeseen absence, Regan Stanford will be taking over her duties on the committee. She'll join Madison Takahashi and myself, of course, thereby bringing the executive board to full capacity again.

I think the new board is the committee's strongest yet. Regan was the brains behind the Hollywood Ball and charity auction, and we've got some superfab ideas in store for the new year. So please do your best to make Reegs feel one hundred and sixty-seven percent welcome.

Besos,
Spencer

2 RESPONSES TO "THE NEW SOCIAL ORDER"

Madison_Ave says: Woo hoo!

QweenKayleen says: OMG, congrats and stuff, Regan. You totally deserve it. You're going to rock in your new position.

QweenKayleen: is so proud of Regan for making executive board even though she's only been at Bradford for a few months and stuff. Super pick, Spencer!

to: Madison_Ave@bradfordprep.com
from: GoldenGirl@bradfordprep.com
date: 12/17, 8:45 p.m.
re: Check This Out

Mads—what do you make of this? I need some insight. Read it and freak.

————————Forwarded Message————————
to: GoldenGirl@bradfordprep.com
from: FrontPaige@bradfordprep.com
date: 12/17, 3:02 p.m.
re: The Thirteenth Step

Hey, Spencer—

I'm kidding, sort of. About this e-mail being the thirteenth step. I mean, we don't actually follow a specific twelve-step program here at Zephyr. They're more into a mind, body, spirit three-tier thing. However, the staff here does like their structure, as I learned the last time I was here, and I've been diligently "working the program" since being checked in. You'd be so proud of me.

(News flash: I haven't exactly had a personality transplant. The aggressive levels of cheer with which everyone walks around here mostly make me want to barf. But working the program is kind of the only way to graduate the program, you know? And God help me, I can't be in here for one moment longer than I have to.)

I don't know if you've spoken to Kaylen, and I know it's kind of hard not to tune out when she's going on and on and *on*— but anyway, life in here is kind of just exactly what you might think from watching a bad reality show.

We're up at the crack of oh-my-jeez doing the teary-eyed self-discovery thing in group. (Side note: You would *hate* the group leader. Think tie-dyed muumuus and Crocs *with socks*. So fugly.) Group is like regular therapy except without the shrink being totally focused on you. Isn't the whole point of therapy about how you get to be the whole entire center of attention? That's what I thought, anyway, but instead, I'm here "sharing" with a Hollywood bimbette who had a nervy b after a botched boob job. *Please.* (Bonus points if you can guess who I'm talking about. I can't say outright. Confidentiality and all.)

So, yeah, group. Early in the morning. I'm not so into it.

Then we've got lunch, which at least is totally organic. (We're allowed to special-order things from the chef. So I'm basically living off of egg white and fat-free goat cheese omelets.) Then it's the one-on-one therapy, *finally*, and then we have crafts. *Crafts.* I'm learning to knit. I know, so *Little House on the Prairie,* but it's better than finger painting or papier-mâché, so please try not to judge.

In the afternoon we have some free time for reading, and I'm finally catching up on my copies of *In Touch.* They do have to approve all of our mail and incoming packages, so sometimes I'm a day or two behind. And there's workout time too. Gunnar Peterson did a special DVD just for me, a mix of cardio-boxing and Krav Maga. As if I wasn't butt-kicking enough before this whole experience, right?

If it sounds like a mini-vacation, don't be fooled. I mentioned group, right? And the early rising? You know I've never been much of a morning person. But I guess it was inevitable that I'd end up here, again, eventually. At least this time I don't have to deal with that backstabbing bitch showing up and screwing up my rehab.

You warned me, Spence, when I started getting in way over my head with my obsession with Regan and revenge. You thought there was something up, that I was headed for some kind of downward spiral, and you were right.

I understand why you did what you did, Spencer—I was out of control. I can't pretend I'm thrilled with the way that things worked out, but I don't blame you. Not anymore. I hope that you don't blame me—too much, anyway. That's part of the whole thirteenth nonstep I was talking about in the first place: making, as the Croc-Monster refers to them, "amends." I am amending, as we speak. Or "e-mending," I guess. Either way, I hope that things can go back to the way that they were when I get out.

Wait, no. Scratch that. Not back to the way that they were. They were all kinds of messed up before I left, after all. So, better than that.

Better than *ever.*

What do you think?

xx,

P

————————End Forwarded Message————————

to: GoldenGirl@bradfordprep.com
from: Madison_Ave@bradfordprep.com
date: 12/17, 9:32 p.m.
re: Check This Out

Holy Gabbana! Well, they say a bad penny always turns up, right?
PS: She sounds a touch pathetic, *non*? With the whole thing about the egg whites and group therapy. Ugh.

---

to: Madison_Ave@bradfordprep.com
from: GoldenGirl@bradfordprep.com
date: 12/17, 9:45 p.m.
re: Check This Out

You don't think there's the slightest chance that she's being sincere?

---

to: GoldenGirl@bradfordprep.com
from: Madison_Ave@bradfordprep.com
date: 12/17, 10:13 p.m.
re: Sincerely

I'll believe it when I see it.

FrontPaige: is mending fences.

 THE BRADFORD BLOG

12/17, 11:08 p.m., by Madison Takahashi

REHAB CHIC

Amy Winehouse, Britney Spears, LiLo . . . their names are synonymous with elegance and class.

LOL, obvs! Opposite Day, anyone?

But if there is anything to be learned from the Holy Trinity of Substance Abuse, it's how *not* to wear your downward spiral on your sleeve . . . or anyplace else on your Lanvin-lovin' person. Fear not, friendlies, with a little attention to detail, you can party to your heart's content without ever compromising your Main Line style.

DON'T: neglect the hair, girlies! Brush and keep on top of your color! Root maintenance is the first thing to go.

DON'T: forget the basics, like eye cream or moisturizer. Puffy eyes and sallow skin are sure symptoms of withdrawal.

DON'T: ever leave the house in your tracksuit. I don't care if it's Juicy Couture. You're better than that, ladies.

3 RESPONSES TO "REHAB CHIC"

GoldenGirl says: Don't forget ragged nails. Ragged nails are a dead giveaway. Or so I read in *Life & Style.*

QweenKayleen says: OMG, Mads! You're so funny! ☺

CaliforniaChic says: Even at my lowest, I was always photoready. Being boho chic has its advantages!

12/18, 3:28 p.m.
privacy setting: ready-to-wear

NATURE ABHORS A VACUUM . . .

I don't know whether this is some kind of willful ignorance or the collective unconscious or what, but somehow, the vibe at Bradford is as though Paige Andrews never even existed to begin with.

And she's only been gone for a week and a half.

Of course, I don't have to tell you guys this. You know. You see it all firsthand. The more things change, the more they stay the same.

Kaylen, for example, is ever the hard-core social climber. E-mailing with Paige back and forth from rehab doesn't seem to be giving her quite the boost she was hoping for; hence, she's got my iPhone on auto-redial. Neediness is the new black. *Not.*

Meanwhile, in the lounge every morning before class, as we hop ourselves up on caffeine (or black tea latte, Spence) and do a quick once-over of one another's wardrobes, there's a kinder, gentler Bradford vibe at work. Like, I can't live without gossip, but tell me the wire doesn't have 20 percent less barb now that Paige and her acid tongue have done a disappearing act. I never knew gossip could be quite so . . . lighthearted. So good-natured. So innocent.

We've still got our fave hangouts and social committee and shopping sprees and cheesy movie nights. What we don't have is Paige. And I kind of don't mind all that much.

High school as the new utopia? I could get used to this.

location: the Closet
status: girl power!
sound track: Gwen, natch

COMMENTS (2):

CaliforniaChic says: I second your emotions.

GoldenGirl says: And I'm making a super-duper special Girl Power playlist. I suspect we'll have many occasions to use it in the near future.

GoldenGirl: is party planning. Everyone get psyched!

 THE BRADFORD BLOG

12/18, 5:24 p.m., by Spencer Kelly

WHEN THE 'RENTS ARE AWAY . . .

. . . the Bradfordians will play.

The parentals will be off vacationing in Anguilla this weekend, so I'd like to announce a small gathering to take place at Casa Kelly on Saturday night. Just a quiet night in, nothing over the top and *certainly* no untoward behavior to be tolerated, but please do dust off your dancing shoes and join us.

Musical suggestions welcome. RSVPs not necessary—you and I both know if you're on the List. A wide array of refreshments will be provided.

Muchos besos, my friendlies. Nine p.m. until we drop. See you there!

xx,

Spence

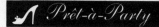

12/20, 5:00 p.m.
privacy setting: ready-to-wear

PRÊT-IER THAN EVER

Girlies, I swear on Zac Posen and all that is good and holy that I am so over school. December and the preholiday rush is the worst-est. Piling on this much work before the break could probably be construed as cruel and unusual punishment, and I, for one, am sick. Of. It. Two papers left until I'm footloose and homework free.

It would probably go faster if I could just put butt in chair and get to it. But that ain't happening. I've got *Project Runway* on the DVR, after all, and my own collection to devise. (Must send off those designs and fabrics to the atelier in Europe soonest so the sewn samples come back in time for me to make adjustments.) Besides, I still have to pick out something fabu to wear to the Kelly manse this evening.

I cannot *wait*. There will be much of the blowing off of steam. It is long overdue. I hope you're both with me on this.

location: the sitting room
status: remote in hand, brain fried
schoolwork: in a state of active neglect. Sue me.

COMMENTS (2):

GoldenGirl says: Finish your papers and get your butt over here, girl! I need you to accessorize for me.

CaliforniaChic says: And don't even try to tell me that you don't have your outfit for tonight ready to go. We know you better than that, *chica*.

2 NEW RESPONSES TO "WHEN THE 'RENTS ARE AWAY . . ."

CatPower says: Wowza, Spence! If that was a small gathering, I can't wait to see what you have in store for your next blowout bash!

FilthyRich says: You said it, dude! Suffice it to say, a good time was had by all. At least, as far as I can recall (which isn't saying much). . . .

✍ Prêt-à-Party

12/21, 2:11 p.m.
privacy setting: private collection

ABOUT LAST NIGHT

That thing that I wrote about needing to blow off steam? Little did I know that Spencer's party was set to explode.

It's a surefire recipe for disaster: Take one hundred or so buttoned-up private school students days away from their winter break (and moments away from their respective personal breaking points) and mix with at least fifteen different types of top-shelf alcohol. Add hormones, pheromones, and all of those other chemicals that apparently get us kids into so much trouble time and again. Blend in a handful of prescription medication used for purely recreational purposes. Stir liberally.

And stand back.

Don't look at me; I don't touch the pills, myself. Between the respective travails of Regan and Paige, I've learned my lesson. But that doesn't mean that I haven't, on occasion, enjoyed my share of mixed drinks in not-entirely-moderate quantities.

Saturday night was no exception. It would have been embarrassing, if sloppiness hadn't, evidently, been the order of the evening.

Take Dalton, for example, who arrived around ten with a cocktail already in hand. (Here's hoping he got a ride over from the family chauffeur.) Carmelita let him in, and he found Regan, Spencer, and me surveying the catered party munchies that Carm had set out on tables. Everything was mostly in order, and we were clustered in that state of prêt-à-party-ness, where the whole evening is stretched out in front of you, you know you're looking fine, you've got a rockin' playlist loaded up, and really, anything could happen.

It's the best, that feeling. Love. It.

"Ladies," Dalton called dramatically, rounding the corner at the top of the staircase, "I'm here. Let the party begin." I tried not to groan out loud.

He had on his Paper Denim & Cloth jeans, dark rinse—which I happen to know for a fact he wears just because he thinks they make his butt look hot—and a sleek dark button-down shirt. The effect was very metro, which I'm sure was just what he'd been going for.

"I'm in need of a refill," Dalton announced, striding over to the bar and handing the glass he'd brought with him to the bartender. "Single-malt scotch. Straight up."

Once replenished, Dalton settled into a seat on the sofa, leering at Regan and almost daring her to join him there. She rolled her eyes at him and sipped her club soda. I wasn't seeing the chemistry, but I never was all that good at science.

The doorbell chimed again, and all at once the house was overflowing with Bradford Prepsters. Kaylen, C.J., Tyler, Toni, Caitlyn, Camden . . . they all showed up, some with friends and all making a beeline for the bar. If I felt weird seeing Tyler all freshly showered, shaved, and dressed for the night, I didn't have time to dwell, thank Gabbana. This being a Bradford party, things got out of control quickly.

The trouble started when Hailey Foster innocently suggested a round of Texas hold 'em. That in and of itself was really no biggie; Regan and I had played a bit at the Oceana, and we were game to buy in. But it wasn't too long before Dalton upped the ante to a game of strip poker. Which, okay, I'm not the shiest girl around, but indecent exposure is really not my thing. Nor is it Regan's—and she was just barely tolerating Dalton's lechy behavior up until this point anyway.

"Thanks, but I'm out," Regan said, tossing her hand down onto the table and gathering her chips.

"You folding?" Dalton asked. "What are you, a prude?" The boy reeked class. And 40-proof alcohol. I could smell it from across the table.

"I'm not folding, I'm cashing out," Regan said. "My body is a wonderland. And you, for one, will never be visiting it."

Hear, hear, sister!

"Whatever." He tried to sound cavalier, but I could see the anger flashing in his eyes. "I don't know why you have to be such a tease, Regan. We all know you were sleeping with Ryder Jared in rehab, so it's not like you can play the V card and act all innocent. Or after that hookup went south and he dumped you on your ass, did you decide to rebound by slumming it up with your poser emo boy toy, Jeremy?"

"Whatevs, Dalton," Regan said, folding her arms across her chest. "For your information, I was the one who broke up with Ryder, not the other way around. But thanks for your concern."

Regan def had my attention now. This was the most I'd ever heard her say on the subject of her relationship with Ryder.

"Everyone knows you're sweating that pathetic geek, Jeremy," Tyler chimed in, his eyes glassy. He'd been hitting the bottle hard since he arrived, matching Dalton *and* C.J. nearly shot for shot. "I mean, he's so deep and brooding. I can't believe you chicks all fall for his act."

At this, Spencer glanced up from her iPod, halfway through her search for a new playlist. She looked displeased, to say the least. As was I.

"You have a real problem, Tyler," she spat. "You need to get over whatever your deal is with Jeremy. The whole thing just makes you look like a jealous freak."

Ouch.

Then again, maybe she was right. Maybe, just maybe, she had a point.

Oh, who am I kidding? *Of course* she was right. I just don't want to admit it, don't want to own up to the fact that Tyler's fixation with Jeremy smacks of Jealous Boyfriend Syndrome. Because that would make Tyler the Jealous Boyfriend, obviously. Which would leave me where, exactly?

I wasn't the only one stung by Spencer's outburst. Tyler stood abruptly. His chair scraped against the floor loudly, echoing throughout the cavernous, cathedral-ceilinged room. He grabbed his crystal tumbler and tossed it with fury. It hit the wall and shattered, raining liquid down onto the imported nineteenth-century hardwood floor planks.

Nice. Way to make yourself seem less jealous, Tyler.

Spencer shook her head with disgust. She leveled Tyler with an icy gaze. "You have a serious problem." She stalked off, presumably to ask Carmelita to clean up the mess.

I pushed myself out of the overstuffed Louis XIV chair I'd been—oh, let's just call it like it was—*hiding* in. I may not be a shrinking violet, but I don't exactly adore conflict. Tyler stood in the center of the room, staring blankly ahead and breathing heavily. Dalton bit his lip while his eyes bore holes in the card table. Regan had taken off after Spencer, Miu Miu stacked heels clacking against the floor in her wake. From the far corner of the room, Hailey and Toni giggled to each other, clutching at champagne bottles and necking them liberally between whispers.

When had things taken such a turn for the ugly?

Fortunately, Spencer's place is way big enough that if a person wants to avoid a large group of awkwardly drunken Bradfordians, one can. Easily. So while Spence and Regan were tending to Tyler's spill, I fled to the screening room.

Spencer and I have spent countless hours in the screening room zoning out to Grace Kelly flicks (her fave) or seventies slasher movies (mine). The two genres make for a really interesting double feature, which has come to be a hallmark of our years-long friendship. Tonight, however, I was savoring the quiet, the blanket of darkness in the room, and the blank movie screen. Despite all of the drama taking place just one floor away, in that room I felt like the only person in the whole freaking house. Possibly even the whole entire world.

Obviously, that feeling couldn't last.

The door creaked open, throwing a patch of light across the center of the room. As the door closed, I relaxed until I heard the intruder walk toward me. Wasn't it obvious that I wanted to be by myself?

"*Excuse* me," I said, "but I came in here so that I could be alone. It sort of kills the whole purpose when people follow me in."

"I was sort of hoping we could be alone together," a voice said softly.

Tyler.

"Nice show out there," I said. I couldn't help myself. "That was a high-class temper tantrum."

Of course it was impossible, but I swear I could actually hear his face flush. "Sorry. I had . . . a moment."

"Yeah, you certainly did." I crossed my legs and sank farther back into the love seat I'd commandeered. I wasn't going to give an inch. He didn't deserve it. He'd chosen Spencer, kept on choosing her with every passing day.

He crossed the room quickly and settled himself next to me. I could feel his breath on my cheek, warm.

Not. Giving. An inch.

"Jealousy is really ugly on you, you know," I said. "Why do you even care about Jeremy so much?"

"I don't know." Tyler shifted in his seat. "It's like a knee-jerk thing."

"You've got the *jerk* part right," I said, glaring.

"I can't help reacting like that. But that doesn't mean it's right. And I know it can't be easy for you."

"None of this is easy for me." An extreme understatement, if ever there was one.

"Me neither." He took my face in one hand and tilted it toward him so that I was looking directly into his eyes. "You know how I feel about you, Maddie. I wish things were different."

"But they're not." Tonight had shown that to me, yet again.

"No," he admitted. "But . . ."

Oh, God. Not a "but." "But" meant that he held out some kind of hope, some possibility that things would change in the future. Which, of course, was totally insane. The best possible outcome for all of us, in this, would be to move on, to let Tyler and Spence ride off into the sunset while I withered away like an old maid in a classic Charles Dickens novel.

Not that I was feeling too sorry for myself or anything. Um, no. Not at all.

I suppose that's why I let myself get swept up in Tyler's "but," in the notion that there might exist some alternate reality in which we'd all come out of this nasty situation unscathed and matched up with our perfect partners. I mean, that would explain my melting, the resolve leaking away like helium from a popped balloon. I slipped closer to Tyler on the love seat, drawn by an invisible force.

Self-pity: It's a dangerous emotion. Second only to lust.

Tyler reached for me, planting butterfly kisses along my neck and shoulder. I sighed and nestled against him.

Then the door flew open again. The shaft of light was back.

I stood up quickly, shakily. "Who's there?" Whoever it was, they could choreograph an MTV VMA performance to the sound of my heartbeat. We were busted. We were *so* busted. What would Spencer say?

"Sorry!" A cascade of giggles shattered the quiet of the room, followed by drunken whispering. "We just wanted to watch, um, *The Philadelphia Story.* Spencer has it, right? In her collection?"

It was Hailey. And Toni. My eyes, now adjusting to the light in the room, darted to the champagne bottles they each clutched. *Okay.* My heartbeat slowed to a waltzlike tempo, which was an improvement. "Yeah, all of the movies are in this closet." I pulled the French doors open to show them. "I can cue the movie up for you. Tyler"—I shot a meaningful look in his direction—"you'd better go find Spencer."

He nodded shortly, looking for a moment as though he was debating saying something. He didn't, though. Instead, after a beat, he just shuffled out of the room.

"Movie!" Toni shrieked, bouncing up and down in her seat like a four-year-old with ADHD.

Right, the *movie.* She wanted to watch a movie. Was drunkenly obsessed with watching a movie. And therefore had little to no idea that she had walked in on something that was every bit as drama-packed as a classic MGM feature. That was fine with me. I was happy to set up a screening for her.

"Okay," I said, picking up the universal remote and passing it along to her.

She squealed, grabbing it from my hand. "Okay."

Okay. We weren't busted, then.

Not this time.

location: bed
hangover level: 6 out of 10
possible ways out of a messy situation: none in sight

---

to: Madison_Ave@bradfordprep.com
from: Ty_It_On@bradfordprep.com
date: 12/21, 3:27 p.m.
re: Checking in

Good afternoon, Maddie,

Are you up and at 'em yet? Last night was pretty hard-core, huh?

I had a good time, though, at the end of it all. At least, I had a good time with you. I hope you had fun too. And don't feel too bad about what happened. We can't help how we feel about each other, right?

Anyway, I just wanted to check in on you, since, y'know, we can't really talk in person the way I'd like to. Are you hanging in today?

Miss you,

Ty

to: Ty_It_On@bradfordprep.com
from: Madison_Ave@bradfordprep.com
date: 12/21, 4:01 p.m.
re: Checking in

Good morning, yourself. I'm hanging in—barely. You're sweet to ask.

I had a good time last night (and a good time with you).

Still wish that things could be different.

XOXO,

Maddie

FilthyRich: never did get to sleep last night. But he did get lucky. Nice!

12/22, 12:32 p.m., by Spencer Kelly

SAY CHEESE!

Or, better yet, just say "congrats"!

You heard it here first, friends: Bradford's own Jeremy Brown has been selected to display his photography at the über-swank Independence Gallery next month.

Jeremy's photos document his year spent in Africa and promise to be much with the moving and thought-provoking, and of course, they're gorgeously shot. Boy's a natural behind the lens.

Stay tuned for details. I, for one, can't wait. And may I add again, yay, Jeremy!

Besos,

Spencer

4 RESPONSES TO "SAY CHEESE!"

CaliforniaChic says: Best. News. Ever. Can't *wait* for your show, Jer. I'm there opening night! ☺

Madison_Ave says: Jeremy! Ah-*mah*-zing news!

QweenKayleen says: Yay, Jeremy!

Ty_It_On says: Nice! I guess it pays to have parents with the right connections.

12/22, 2:16 p.m.
privacy setting: private collection

WONDER GIRL

Having just seen the Bradford blog about Jeremy's photography show, I just can't help but wonder:

WTF is Tyler's deal?

Yeah, I know that Spencer's history with Jeremy is annoying to Tyler, but come on. If he, like any normal person with eyes in their head, can tell that there's still mad chemistry brewing between those two, well then . . . technically, shouldn't he be *glad*?

You know, maybe not doing backflips or taking out yearbook ads about it or anything, but if Spencer and Jeremy found their way back to each other, then that would free things up for Tyler and me to get together, no harm, no foul.

And isn't that what he wants? Isn't that what we *both* want?

I thought so. Now I'm not so sure.

Unless . . . maybe all of the recent tensions between Tyler and Spencer just prove that they're continuing to grow farther and farther apart. In which case, it should be a mere matter of time before he and I are free and clear to be together once and for all.

I guess you could call that a silver lining.

Joy.

location: the Bradbrary
status: suitably green-eyed
sound track: someone has tuned the radio to a "soft rock"
   station. Bad news. Rock should never be soft.

12/22, 6:18 p.m.
privacy setting: private collection

MAIN LINE'S MOST WANTED

How many not-totally-legal incidents does it take to technically qualify as a crime spree? Two? Three? More?

I need to know, seriously. I need concrete parameters for "spreeage."

Because it happened again. Just like the first time, with the sunglasses. Only easier now. And even more fun, if I'm being completely honest with myself.

I have the flask.

And no idea how, when, or if it's even possible to give it to Tyler.

I didn't go back to the jewelry store with the plan of shoplifting anything. When I left my house, I actually didn't have *any* plan at all, other than to take a quick study break before my poor, dehydrated brain shriveled up inside my skull completely. (Hangovers are not super conducive to cram sessions, I'm discovering. Go figure.)

I swear, I only meant to indulge in a quick drive-by, maybe find and purchase—"purchase" being the operative word here— a new scarf from Bebe or those Prada mary janes that Regan told me she thought would look cute with that cream-colored satin jumpsuit I rescued from Destroyed Girl. That was all. But as I walked down Walnut, I found myself walking inside Jack Kellmer—just to check, to see if the flask was still there, I told myself. Maybe it had already sold, making my decision for me.

It wasn't there.

The case was empty. Problem solved. I realized I'd been holding my breath, and I let it out in one big *whoosh.*

"What are you doing here?"

I sucked all of the air in the store back in again.

It was Spencer. Standing at the jewelry counter, admiring those black pearl earrings from our last shopping trip as they danced against her golden highlights. On her wrist she wore the cuff bracelet I'd noticed the last time we were in the store.

I allowed myself a quick glance: The flask sat on the counter, smooth against its velvet backdrop. Not gone. Just relocated. Awesomeness.

The air around me ionized again.

"I was just taking a break, you know? I'm fried," I stammered.

She nodded. "I'm so with you on that. But you should have called me. I would have played hooky with you."

I laughed, my voice sounding too shrill, too loud in my own ears. "I wanted to—" How to finish that sentence? "I was looking for your Christmas present."

Good save, Mads. Very very veriness.

Spencer's face split into a wide, genuine smile. "You're the sweetest. I'll pretend I never saw you here. I'm supergood at acting surprised." She made a big show of gluing her eyes shut and rotating her body away from me.

I bit my lip, thinking. The salesclerk was nowhere to be found—probably in the back, checking on some stock for Spencer. The flask, however, was just sitting there. And Spencer wasn't even looking.

"You're a good friend, Princess Grace," I said, my voice wavering. I scooped up the flask, slipped it into the pocket of my wool Tahari car coat, and clapped her on the shoulder. "I'll come back later. And just remember: I'm a size four."

location: the Closet
manicure: gnawed off
Christmas shopping list: still pretty long. But at least I know what I'm giving Tyler. That is, if I don't chicken out.

12/23, 12:08 p.m., by Kaylen Turner

PLAYING YOU HOT AND COLD

Hey, Bradfordians:

Clearly, you shouldn't need a reminder about one of the hottest (and chillest) social events of the season, but just in case you are suffering from a head trauma and stuff, a note:

This year's annual Fire and Ice Ball will be held on Christmas Eve at Saketini. It'll be our last major blowout before everyone departs for winter break, so make yourself pretty and make yourself present!

Rooftop views, DJ Romeo spinning, and signature cocktails flowing freely. *And,* since certain fallen idols can't be here to join us, we're going to have to make our own fun. Please plan your scandals accordingly.

Besos, babes,

QweenK

2 RESPONSES TO "PLAYING YOU HOT AND COLD"

CatPower says: Can't wait to rawk it on the rooftop!

CaliforniaChic says: Um, excuse me? Stealing Spencer's sign-off, are we, Kaylen? Lame, very lame. You're lucky Paige isn't around to see this. Then again, if she were here, *she'd* be the one posting about the party, right?

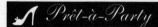

12/23, 2:21 p.m.
privacy setting: private collection

THE PLOT THICKENS

The following is a transcript of sorts. I'm saving it for when I'm a famous international designer and they make a documentary of my formative years. You never know what sort of material they'll be looking for, and this drama is *way* hot.

What? It could totally happen.

CHARACTERS:

Madison Takahashi

Spencer Kelly

Regan Stanford

Jeremy Brown

INT. BRADFORD LOUNGE
REGAN, MADISON, and SPENCER are sprawled catty-cornered in the main seating area of the lounge. Regan files her nails while Spencer sips at a green tea and Madison thumbs through an issue of W.

REGAN
(not looking up from her nails, which are
neon yellow and, of course, impeccable)
Is anyone actually done with their papers yet?

SPENCER AND MADISON
(in unison)
Nope.

REGAN
They're really going to drag this out until the
bitter end, huh? Keep us working until the second
before the last bell rings before vacation?

SPENCER AND MADISON
(again in unison)
Yup.

REGAN
Very cute, you guys. Did you practice that?

SPENCER AND MADISON
(still together)
Don't need to.

All three girls look up and laugh. Around the corner comes JEREMY,
messenger bag slung over his shoulder and looking distracted.

REGAN
Jeremy!

He makes his way over to the group.

JEREMY
Didn't figure you three for class cutters.

SPENCER AND MADISON
(in unison)
Study hall.

JEREMY
(unfazed; he knows from Spencer and Mads's history, of course)
Right.

REGAN sits up in her seat and flips her hair over one shoulder.

REGAN
So, are we still on for this evening?

REGAN turns toward the girls.

REGAN (cont.)
Jeremy's going to give me a sneak peek of the pics that are being featured in the Independence Gallery show.

SPENCER
(a tad wistfully)
That's right. I totally never got to congratulate you in person. It's so fantastic that you're getting to show your work.
(a beat, thoughtful)
I always knew your photography was amazing.

JEREMY is quiet for a moment, then:

JEREMY
Thanks. You've always been so supportive,
Spence. I really appreciate it.
(Looks at his watch)
Man—I've gotta go. Not all of us have study hall this period.
(to Regan)
Meet me in the parking lot after school?

REGAN
Definitely.

*As he walks away, Madison and Regan turn toward Spencer,
eyebrows raised.*

SPENCER
What? *What?*
(sighing)
Okay, yeah, so, I'm more confused than ever.

REGAN
Shocker.

MADISON
I totally had no idea.

SPENCER
(rolling her eyes)
It gets better, though.

MADISON
Better than the two of you having eye-sex
with each other right here in the school lounge
during study hall and making your bestest friends dodge
the flying drool? I can't even imagine.

SPENCER
Well, okay, I guess by "better," I actually meant "worse."

REGAN
Are we speaking in riddles now?

SPENCER
It's just . . . I feel like Tyler might be slipping away from me.
And, like, I know I'm all confused and stuff with Jeremy, but
the thing is that the weirder everything gets with Tyler, the
more I realize that I do still have strong feelings for him too. I
have too many feelings! I'm a slut. I'm a feelings-slut!

REGAN
Or a normal girl with a little drama in her love life.

SPENCER
Great, and while I try to untangle everything,
Tyler just floats farther and farther out of my grasp.
I don't even know what's going on with us lately.
(tentative)
You guys . . . you guys don't think there's someone else,
do you? Like, that Tyler might be going behind my back?

MADISON is flustered, knocks her magazine off of her lap
and onto the floor, spraying subscription cards everywhere.

MADISON
What? Tyler? Cheat? No way.
(shakes her head)
No. Way.

REGAN *bends over to collect Madison's magazine detritus.*

REGAN
Try switching to decaf, dearie.
(turning to Spencer)
I mean . . . I don't think so. At least, I've never heard
anything about it or noticed anyone else he's into. But it's not
like he'd be sharing that info with me, you know?

MADISON
That's so not even the point. He doesn't have anything *to*
share! Tyler adores you, Spence. But what I don't get is
why this is even an issue. You know, sometimes couples
drift apart. It's sad, but it happens. Why don't you, you
know, follow your heart? I know it's a cheesy greeting-card
expression, but there's a kernel of truth behind every cheesy
greeting-card expression. Meaning that you sweat Jeremy
and, therefore, you should totally get with him.

REGAN
I'm not sure—

MADISON
Come *on,* Regan. Even if you guys did hook up or
whatever at the beginning of the semester, you have to
see that Spencer plus Jeremy equals true lurve.

REGAN

We never hooked up! *Ew!* I mean not *ew* exactly, but, like—
we're friends. Total friends. Have always been friends. In the
friendly, non-naked way. *Gawd.* But anyway, I just think . . .
Jer's a sensitive soul, you know? And I can't help but look out
for him. If you really want to be with him, Spence, you know I
support you. But don't mess with his head.
He doesn't deserve that.

MADISON

I just think you need to make up your mind already.

SPENCER
(surprised)
Um, okay.
(uncertain pause)
Will do, Mads.

MADISON forces a laugh.

MADISON

That came out weird. Obvs you should do
what's best for you. Whatever that is.
(changing the subject)
Like, for example, if what was best for Regan was toying with
the dirtiest mind of the junior class, that would be cool.

REGAN

Huh? You mean Dalton? Please. I have to admit
he's fairly hot, but def not boyfriend material.

SPENCER

But you admit to an ongoing battle of wits?

REGAN

I admit nothing! I mean, I can see how you might pick up the teensiest little spark there or something. But that's it! Just a little verbal sparring here and there. Nothing bearing even the slightest resemblance to a relationship of any sort. I'm definitely on a relationship hiatus at the moment.

MADISON

Bitterness! Details, please.

REGAN

Boys are more trouble than they're worth. I learned that back in Cali. The hard way. So, for now, verbal sparring is enough for me.

MADISON

Huzzah for the verbal sparring!

SPENCER

You girls are crazy.

REGAN

And about to be late to class.

They stand, straighten their clothes, and collect their books and belongings. As they disappear down the hallway, Spencer tosses her empty cup into a garbage can and hip checks Madison playfully. All is well and secret remains safe. For now.

And, *scene.*

location: lit class. Teach thinks I'm freewriting! Hee!
status: ready for my close-up
friendships: still intact

12/23, 3:18 p.m.
privacy setting: ready-to-wear

DONE AND DONE!

Friendlies!

I am pleased to inform you that as of 3:03 this afternoon, I am hereby officially done with my schoolwork for this semester and have made massive progress on my spring collection! And not a moment too soon. There was a point back there when I thought my head was going to catch fire atop my sad, overburdened little shoulders. Which would have *really* ruined my rad 3.1 Phillip Lim tuxedo blouse.

So all's well that ends well.

Please join me tonight for some quality vegging at Casa Takahashi. But no major pigging out—we need to look fantabulous for tomorrow night, after all. I have some sugar-free Jell-O that should hit the spot.

I'm off. Have certain important business to attend to: i.e., the final touches on my smokin' dress for the big ball.

Mwah!
Mads

location: my car—updating at a stoplight.
status: free as a bird. Jealous, girlies?
tuxedo blouse: hott. Duh.

COMMENTS (2):

GoldenGirl says: I'm there. I'll bring the low-carb lollipops.

CaliforniaChic says: So I guess that means I've got the SmartWater?

GoldenGirl: is starving. Must find the carrot sticks. *Carrot sticks.* Sigh. The things we do for beauty. . . .

Ty_It_On: Hey, gorgeous.

Madison_Ave: Flattery will get you everywhere.

Ty_It_On: ☺

Ty_It_On: Did u have a fun nite?

Madison_Ave: Totally. We watched *Dial M for Murder,* old episodes of *The O.C.,* and we ate inappropriate quantities of sugar-free Red Vines. Always a good time.

Ty_It_On: Please tell me pillow fights in lingerie factored into your fun.

Madison_Ave: Sorry, but we don't actually live in a *Playboy* centerfold. Anyway, I'm sure u heard about all of this already from Spencer.

Ty_It_On: Oh, ouch.

Madison_Ave: It's the truth, right?

Ty_It_On: No comment.

Madison_Ave: Exactly.

Ty_It_On: Let's just concentrate on fun, happy stuff—like how awesome tomorrow night will be.

Madison_Ave: Will it?

Ty_It_On: I wouldn't expect any less.

Madison_Ave: And as for me?

Ty_It_On: ???

Madison_Ave: What can I expect? From u?

Ty_It_On: OK, I'm sensing some tension here.

Madison_Ave: Really? You don't say.

Ty_It_On: Really really. What gives? Did I do something wrong?

Madison_Ave: <sigh> No, I guess not. But you're being all flirty and cute and whatnot, and it's not going to work.

Ty_It_On: No?

Madison_Ave: I am making a resolution. This is me, resolving: This is it.

Ty_It_On: U sound serious.

Madison_Ave: I am serious. Serious as a Badgley Mischka sample sale.

Ty_It_On: So, that's it, then?

Madison_Ave: Look, we can be . . . whatever we are. We can be together. If.

Ty_It_On: Tell me. Whatever you want. Say the word. Seriously.

Madison_Ave: If you break it off with Spencer.

Madison_Ave: ?

Madison_Ave: Clearly, I lost you there.

Madison_Ave: OK, bye.

Ty_It_On: No! You didn't lose me. I was just thinking. I mean, Spence and I have been 2gether for a while now. A person doesn't just make these decisions lightly.

Madison_Ave: Right. As I was saying: Bye now.

Ty_It_On: Will you chill for a sec? God! I understand what you're getting at, and the sneaking around, it's not cool. So, you're right. I'm going to do it.

Madison_Ave: Do what?

Ty_It_On: End it with Spencer. So that u and I can be 2gether, 4 real.

Madison_Ave: . . .

Ty_It_On: I was expecting some more enthusiasm here, Maddie.

Madison_Ave: I'll be plenty enthusiastic. When you do it.

Ty_It_On: U don't believe me?

Madison_Ave: Give me a reason 2.

Ty_It_On: I will.

Madison_Ave: I'm waiting. . . .

Ty_It_On: isn't loving the hard choices.

12/24, 5:11 p.m.
privacy setting: private collection

NERVES OF NOODLES

I'm starting to wonder how long, exactly, a person can spend walking the world feeling like she could, at any moment, spontaneously spew massive chunks of uncontrollable barfitude across the unsuspecting public. I mean, surely this nerves-driven nausea has to subside at some point, right?

Right?

I can't take this any longer. Something's got to give. Either Tyler and Spencer need to break up, as Ty promises is coming, or I need to meet someone else, stat (which is not a very girl-powery solution, I know, but I'm desperate here, so let's all get on board, mmmkay?).

In the meantime, I'm throwing myself full force into designing my collection for Destroyed Girl. (I *must* send everything off to the atelier before I leave for Aspen so I get the samples back in time to make adjustments and add special touches.) Perhaps focusing on vintage fabrics and fashion trends will distract me from the emotional roller coaster I'm on right now. So far, it's not really working. I'm designing some great pieces, but I can't shake the constant obsession with Tyler and the guilt over what we did.

The fact is, I wouldn't feel so conflicted about my feelings for Tyler if Spencer weren't the bestest bestie in the Kingdom of Bestiedom. And, all of my inner turmoil aside, things are only getting bestier between us.

Wretchedness.

Allow me to explain: This afternoon she came by my house to model our Fire and Ice outfits and have our hair done for tonight (we heart a good dress rehearsal, and it's important to be well coiffed). Mom managed to snag Garren for the day; he owed her a favor from back when Dad catered a Fashion Week after-party of his (connections are *so* very). Regan joined us, and there was a flurry of activity of and relating to Bespoke T3 tourmaline flat irons, Bumble and Bumble styling crème, and ornate hair accessories crafted by yours truly.

Once we were sufficiently beautified, Regan flitted off, babbling something about an appointment at Moko in Old City. Girl is *such* a sucker for organic products and what-have-you. But then again, that's why we love her, the skinny little bohemian.

And then it was just me and Spencer. Spencer and me. Alone. Like old times. Normally, I'd say that we make a fairly fearsome twosome, but today there was an interloper among us: the aforementioned nerves-driven nausea that Wouldn't. Leave. Me. Alone. And it came with its own plus-one; namely, a heavy dose of conscience on the side.

Despite what's going on within the confines of my internal organs, I will always love hanging with Spencer. She still tells me *everything,* no matter how excruciating the full disclosure can be to my ego. It's like she hasn't even noticed (or, maybe, doesn't want to notice) that anything has changed, that something's up. With me. With us.

So, you know: blessing + curse = Mads stressed to the maximus.

Blech.

To wit, allow me to paint you a tableau of friendship: *feminiculus grandus*. The scene: this afternoon, my bedroom.

"What do you think's going to happen when Paige gets sprung from druggie jail?" Spencer asked me, innocently enough. She was sprawled (carefully, so as not to destroy her intricate side ponytail, especially now that Garren and his posse were halfway back to NYC) on my bed, clicking through a photo album on my MacBook.

I glanced over her shoulder. No wonder she'd asked about Paige—she was looking at pictures from the Hollywood Ball. The night Spence'd done us all a favor and had the lunatic bizznatch sent away.

The night I stabbed her right in the center of her delicate porcelain back. The night that Tyler and I had sex.

"Paige coming back? I can see it now: The world will rotate backward on its axis. The rivers will run with blood. Lions, lambs, *Project Runway* getting booted from the fall television lineup. End-of-days sort of stuff."

"So, badness?" Spencer flipped the laptop shut and looked up at me. "That's the upshot that we're looking at here?"

"Badness," I repeated. "Of the baddiest variety. We're talking about Paige Andrews, remember?"

Spencer sighed heavily. "I know you're right. I guess I'm just in denial or something. Things have been so great lately with you, me, and Regan that I don't want to think about anything upsetting the social order."

"Paige thinks she *is* the social order," I said.

"I wish we could freeze time so it could stay just like this forever."

"But then we'd never get to wear our pretty dresses to the Fire and Ice Ball," I replied. There was no way I was going to miss an opp to model a Glamourista original. Please, people. Also: Garren-hair.

Spencer threw a pillow at me, hitting me squarely in the stomach, which didn't do a whole lot to help all of the lurching going on in there. Clearly, Spencer thinks that things are perfect with us, that life is happiness and rainbows and a front-page spread in *Vogue* for my spring collection.

If only she knew. If only it were.

"Hey," she chirped, snapping me out of my trance. "Are these the earrings you're going to wear tonight? I don't remember them. Where'd you get these?" She scooped up the Jennifer Meyer hammered-gold discs that lay on my nightstand.

"Uh—probably," I hedged, caught off guard. "I picked them up at Touché." It was the truth. Indeed, the earrings were from Touché. And I had literally picked them up there. So what if I was omitting the fact that I'd then dropped them into my pocket and quickly walked out the front door?

"I might find something else that I like better with my outfit," I stammered, praying to the gods of Dolce & Gabbana that she wouldn't notice my lurching stomach, pounding heart, and suddenly clammy hands. I'd been so paranoid during that particular snatch-and-grab that I'd fully expected the salesclerk to stop me at the door. I was certain that the manager made deliberate eye contact because she was about to bust me, but then she wished me a pleasant day and the salesclerk held the door open for me. Still, it was nauseating. That creepy feeling had partially killed the buzz I'd come to crave from these little adventures. Now it was making me way flustered and more than a little worried that I might spontaneously blurt out a confession.

"Do you know what they remind me of?" she mused.

"Nope." My heart was beating so loud, it could have pounded that gold into submission all by its lonesome. Egad.

"The necklace that Tyler bought me for my birthday last spring. Remember? It was the same shape, but I think . . . platinum?"

She *thought* platinum. Platinum, she thought. I made a mental note that if and when Tyler and I ever reached the point where we were free to publicly exchange jewelry or other forms of gifts, I would damn well burn the memory of each and every token of his love into my brain for all eternity. There would be no thinking. There would be *certainty*.

No wonder they're drifting apart.

Still, I tried to remain as neutral as possible, given the circumstances. "I know which necklace you mean. It was so pretty. Why don't you wear it anymore?"

She shrugged. "That's a good question. I don't know. I guess it's just that we've been together for long enough that there was always something new to model. You know?"

"Could be worse," I commented lightly.

"I know." She bit her lip. "See, I've been doing a lot of thinking."

Thinking. Thinking was good. Thinking could lead to acting, and acting could lead to dumping, which could in turn lead to moving on. Which, you know, might mean that Tyler and I would be free to be together and do the whole boyfriend-girlfriend gift exchange thing and etc.

"Tell me," I proposed.

"It's just . . . after we talked the other day, I realized that you're right—I do have feelings for Jeremy."

"Right." Yay!

"But."

But. But? "But" was no good. "But" wouldn't amount to boyfriendliness and hammered-gold whatnot from Tyler in my foreseeable future. (NOT that this is about hammered-gold whatnot. Hammered-gold whatnot is merely an enjoyable by-product of the state of legitimate girlfriendment.)

"But what?" I asked, dreading her response.

"But . . . I still love Tyler."

"Really?" *Really?*

"Really."

I exhaled loudly. "Well, that's good, I guess."

She peered at me.

"That you know how you feel." *Even if it is exactly the opposite of how I want you to feel.*

"And, you know, who even knows what's going on with Jeremy. Feelings aren't entirely *reliable,* right?"

"They aren't?" I caught her look. "They aren't. Definitely. Are not."

"Tyler, though . . . *Tyler* is reliable. Our relationship is reliable. So I think . . . I'm going to stick with it. With the, um, sure thing." She sounded so sure of herself. Not.

"How romantic," I croaked. Reliability. That's not exactly what was drawing *me* to Tyler.

Her confession over, Spence smoothed the bedspread out underneath her fingers and smiled. "I got him the thing." I seriously hoped "thing" wasn't code for something sexy. I was for sure going to vomit on her if she was about to tell me that she'd bought him handcuffs or something like that. A girl can take only so much.

"Thing?"

"The flask. From Rittenhouse. Oh—that's right. You left before I could point it out."

I felt like someone had dropped my heart into a trash compactor: flat, mangled. It hadn't even occurred to me that she'd seen the flask, had realized how perfect it would be for Tyler. Silly me.

"Oh?" I coughed. "Oh," I repeated, more loudly this time.

"Yeah, it's perfect for him." She brushed an artfully arranged blond tendril out of her eye. "So I went back to the store yesterday and got one. I got it engraved for him and everything."

"It sounds perfect," I said softly. And it did. Way more perfect than the flask that I'd stolen. I couldn't give that to him now, of course. But I couldn't return it to the store, either, since I obviously didn't have a receipt. It looked like I was keeping the flask for myself.

Merry Christmas, Mads.

"Oh—and when I told him that I'd gotten him his gift, he got so excited, Maddie," Spencer was saying. Her voice was all bubbly, and she was doing that little lisp that happens when she wins a game in field hockey or eats too much processed sugar. "He made a plan for us to go out to dinner together for a private gift exchange."

Spencer gets taken to dinner, I get taken to bathrooms and backseats. Enough said. Who have I been kidding, thinking Tyler would dump her for me?

"And he said he couldn't decide between Tangerine and Bistro St. Tropez, but then I suggested Fountain, because it's actually in the Four Seasons, and that way, you know . . ." She waggled her eyebrows at me and let her voice trail off meaningfully.

I looked up and realized her eyebrows had frozen mid-waggle. Oh no.

"Mads? What's going on? You're looking sort of . . . green."

"Green?" Never a good sign. I am known for my rosy cheeks, as a general rule.

"You'd better not be coming down with something! We have Fire and Ice tonight!" As if I could forget. She leaped up from the bed and rushed to me, holding out the back of her hand like a worried mother.

I ducked from underneath her touch. "I'm fine, I swear. I just haven't eaten enough today."

Spencer squeezed my wrist. "Well, grab a snack so you don't faint. Tonight is going to be so great."

I nodded slowly. "It will."

I told myself that I wasn't lying. It *was* going to be a great night. Spencer was going to have an amazing time. Her boyfriend was busting out the red carpet for her, had an A-list Christmas planned for her, and was definitely going to sweep her off her feet. I wasn't worried about Spencer one bit.

Myself?

Well, that was a different matter entirely.

location: the kitchen
status: Tums-ified
upcoming dinner dates at the Fountain Four Seasons: zero

12/25, 1:11 a.m.
privacy setting: private collection

BREAKING UP IS REALLY, REALLY, REALLY HARD TO DO

Especially when, technically, you and the breakup-ee aren't even really together.

I did try, though. You have to give me points for that. An A for effort. So what if I got an F in execution? (Okay, so maybe it was actually more like an F minus, if we're going to be strictly honest here.)

Well, if I had to crash and burn, I suppose there was no better place to do it than at the Fire and Ice Ball. At least I went down in flames while dressed to the nines. The truth is that after hearing from Spencer how Tyler had just gone all loverboy on her, I was totally resolved to be Over Him, rather than All Over Him. And, as they say, looking good is the best revenge. (Well, that, and making out with some hot male-model DJ-type in plain sight of the jackass who broke your heart. Luckily, the ball provided opportunity for both.)

My outfit kicked ass, natch. I had the "fire" part covered with some seriously hot black satin formal shorts (I know—shorts! At a ball! Can you believe it?) and a one-shouldered draped halter top in a paint-the-town shade of red. Over the halter I slung a chain belt embellished with Swarovski crystals. I topped (or should I say, bottomed?) the whole thing off with silver cutout YSL bondage booties. I fastened some earrings in, deciding to eschew the purloined pair that Spence had been fingering earlier. The contraband aspect of them wasn't sitting so well with me right now, and anyway, there'd be plenty of other chances to bust them out again when the guilt wasn't feeling quite so fresh. Then I took a long, hard look at myself in the full-length along the wall of the Closet.

Perfection.

I knew Tyler would be sweating me tonight. And if I couldn't have him—if he wasn't, in fact, going to break up with Spencer as he'd promised me that he would—well then, I'd settle for him wanting me and not getting what he wanted.

Tyler *hates* not getting what he wants.

Ooh, Spence just texted a pic from the ball. Ouch. Some people—like, namely, Joanna Moore people—need to not go the strapless route. Like, *ever.* I mean, not without some serious Pilates-fying. I'm sorry, not trying to be too blitch-tastic, but it's true. I've got the visual aids to prove it. I *have just seen the film.* It's called the Reformer, Joanna—look into it. Or alternatively? Kimono sleeves. They are your friends!

But what was I saying before the tragic pic arrived?

Oh, right. Me = hotness. Nary a bat arm in sight, I can say with confidence. Not that my rockin' muscle-toned entrance seemed to have any effect on Tyler and Spencer. They were too busy swallowing each other's faces when I arrived to really take note.

The ball itself was, as Tyler would say, *en fuego*: The walls of Saketini were done up in satiny strips of blazing reds and oranges (and, in fact, were probably a fire hazard, ironically enough, but whatevs), and the floor was translucent and lit up like something out of a bad seventies John Travolta movie in what I'm thinking was meant to be an approximation of ice. No matter, it looked cool (no pun intended, swearsies).

Unfortunately, Tyler looked cool too. *And* hot. At least, as much of him as I could see from his lip-locked position adjacent to the bar. To stand there, lurking ten feet away from the two of them—my best friend and her boyfriend—was most definitely creepy, and more than a little suspicious. Watching them together made me feel like I'd swallowed a book of matches. That had gone down lit. But I couldn't tear myself away from the train wreck in front of me.

So much for entertaining the idea that this mess could possibly have a happy ending for me.

"Mads, you are *rawking* those shorts!"

I whirled to find it was Kaylen clutching at my arm, her fingertips wet and cold from the cocktail she'd been sucking down. She grabbed two more from a passing waitress and handed one over to me. Judging from the glassy-eyed grin she was giving me, this wasn't her first refill.

"Thanks," I said. "That's quite a jumpsuit." It was Versace and meant for someone six times her age. Or possibly living in a different decade.

Kaylen flushed. "Thanks. I was trying to be different."

"Mission accomplished," I said, raising an eyebrow.

Regan swooped in and bore down on Kaylen affably, wrapping an arm around her shoulder. Her dress, shorter than what she usually wore, was Grecian-style and draped gracefully across her lanky torso. Girl can seriously frock out, I tell you, and the sunflower shade of the satin accented the gold highlights in her hair. Or maybe the glow that I saw surrounding her was just me projecting, seeing as how she was a guardian angel rescuing me from Kaylen.

Kaylen means well—I *think*. Well, sometimes she does, anyway—but I so didn't have the energy tonight. It was all I could do not to wrap one of those strips of fabric adorning the walls around Tyler's neck and squeeze. And I still had to pretend like everything was all normal when the insides of my stomach were reenacting that Munch painting that they sell at every single poster shop on South Street, *The Scream.*

"I think Camden was looking for you, Kay," Regan said, shaking her curls back off of her shoulder. "Over by the karaoke booth."

Kaylen nodded and scurried off. "Laters!" she promised.

I looked at Regan. "There's a karaoke booth?"

She shrugged. "There's a *something* booth. Maybe it's karaoke. Maybe it's a psychic. Maybe it's a Porta Potty. I don't know. But her jumpsuit was giving me a headache."

I giggled. "Mean!"

"Come on. She's so fake! You know she just reports everything back to Paige, anyway." Suffice it to say, Regan is not exactly a fan of Paige. Not that I blame her one bit.

"You're right." I glanced up just in time to see Tyler lean over and whisper something into Spencer's ear. She blushed and smiled at him.

"What are you ogling?" Regan followed my gaze. "Ugh, I *know*—can't they, like, get a room? They've been molesting each other since they got here. I mean, I know 'tis the season, but still. Time and place." She smiled to show me she was mostly kidding. "Or maybe Spence has, like, mistletoe tucked into that tiara of hers. Little minx."

I tried to smile back.

Spencer caught my eye and waved happily. Her skin glowed like an ad for a Bliss spa refining fruit acid wash facial. She had embraced the theme of the evening by frosting herself in about forty pounds of ice in the form of the Kelly diamonds; she broke those out only on ultraspecial occasions. Obviously, she was feeling extra romantical and fancy-schmancy tonight. There was a tiara involved, albeit an understated one. (There's only so understated a tiara can be, anyway.)

At least I didn't see any mistletoe, from where I stood.

I forced a grin and turned back to Regan. "Should we karaoke?" Something, *anything* to put a little bit of space between myself and Spyler.

Regan raised an eyebrow. "Screaming off-key Rihanna? You're better than that. And that's assuming it even is a karaoke booth and not a Porta Potty. No *way* am I singing lame-ass pop music with you in a bathroom stall made of plastic. First you sip. Then we dance."

What could I do? I sipped my signature drink, the one that Daddy created for me: a ginger-champagne cocktail garnished with actual bits of dried ginger (quite *yum*). We danced, and for a short while, at least, I even found myself having (could it actually be?) *fun.*

Clearly, it wasn't to last.

What is it about two girls dancing that makes boys get all sweaty and hopped up so they feel like they have to intrude? And why—oh, why—is it always the wrong boys?

In this case, the aforementioned DJ and Dalton.

In the DJ's defense, he was a great kisser, as I discovered while making out with him in the middle of the dance floor. His main fault, as far as this evening was concerned, was that he simply isn't Tyler. And meanwhile, Regan had already witnessed Dalton putting his smarmtastic moves on Camden Barrett again earlier in the evening, and she wasn't all that interested in his particular brand of dirty dancing. A few minutes of the four of us bobbing together along the disco-fever dance floor, and Regan was winding herself backward while Dalton tried unsuccessfully to follow. For my part, the flashing lights were starting to give me a headache. I hoped I wasn't going to have a strobe-induced seizure or something. That certainly wouldn't tip the Tyler scales in my favor.

The dance floor was packed, but there was no sign of Spencer and Tyler. And I was So. Not. Having. Any. of this. I waved at the DJ, mouthed some random excuse to Regan (who in turn went off in search of Jeremy on the roof-deck), and bowed out of our little group. Air. I needed air.

But first I needed to pee.

It being a Takahashi club, the bathrooms were extra large and tiled in imported marble. Daddy always makes sure every inch of his places are super luxurious. I ducked inside the ladies' to find that both stalls (private rooms with slatted doors that reached two thirds of the way down to the floor) were occupied. Based on the aggressive sniffing sounds coming from at least one of the stalls, I decided to give the room's occupants their privacy. Paige's drug bust was bad enough—I know better than to get within ten feet of that particular type of drama these days.

I stepped back out of the restroom so hastily that I barely took in my surroundings. Which, in this case, was problematic, as I suddenly found myself entangled with none other than Tyler himself. In fact, I nearly ground my pointy heel into his pinky toe. Accidentally, of course, but I'd be lying if I said it didn't please me slightly to watch him wince.

"Ouch," he said. "There are easier ways to keep me off the dance floor." He smirked that tiny upturned grin of his that said everything I didn't want to hear right now. Pop Rocks went off in my stomach.

"I wasn't trying to cripple you, Tyler. It's not your *dancing* that's got me pissed off." I arched an eyebrow at him meaningfully.

"I pissed you off?" He actually managed to look surprised. I swear, he must have practiced that expression in the mirror, that perfect mixture of shock, dismay, and concern. It was just that good. The concern part was what got me, sincere or no. God help me, as much as I wanted to be, I wasn't totally impervious to it.

Pop Rocks. Popping.

I didn't even know where to begin. I dragged him a few steps down the hallway and around a corner so we'd be a little more stealth.

"Yes, you pissed me off," I spat. "You told me—you *promised*—that you were going to end things with Spencer." My voice hitched, just a small catch at the back of my throat, but a hitch, no doubt about it. I gritted my teeth in an effort not to cry. He would *not* see me cry over him. Especially not while I was wearing silver-tipped false eyelashes. I certainly wasn't going to let a *guy* come between myself and ocular fierceness.

"And that's obviously not going to happen. So, I mean, okay, fine"—well, not fine at *all*, really, but what was there left for me to say?—"but if that's the case, then it's over between us. For real. For good. I'm not sneaking around behind my best friend's back." I glared at him. "Spencer deserves better than that. And so do I."

I realized, almost to my own disbelief, that I actually meant what I was saying, which helped to keep the weepiness at bay. It's not just what I've been doing to Spencer, though of course that's a *huge* part of the wrongness of this situation. But it's what I've been doing to *myself*—pretending that I was okay with being someone else's second choice, a dirty little secret. I believe that Tyler cares about me . . . he just doesn't care about me *enough.*

"I have to go. Your girlfriend will notice if I disappear for too long." I pivoted on one stiletto heel, prepared to stalk off, but he caught me by the elbow and twirled me back around so that I was facing him again.

"Mads, you're upset, I get it," he said.

"Gee, thanks for being so *understanding*," I snapped.

"No," he stammered, frustrated, which I have to admit, I found endearing. What is *wrong* with me?

Must. Stay. Strong. Eyelashes. Remember the eyelashes.

"I'm saying this all wrong. What I mean is, *of course* you're upset. This is a really lousy situation. And you're in the worst position of all of us here. And maybe I haven't been sensitive enough to that, you know?"

I shrugged. "Maybe."

"But it's not because I don't care. I *do*." He pulled me closer. "Madison, don't you understand how badly I want us to be together?"

Eye. Lashes.

"I swear to you, I am going to break up with Spencer as soon as it is humanly possible. But I can't do it right now—I mean, tomorrow's Christmas, for chrissakes. And then we all leave for Aspen, and if I do it now, it'll make things messy and awkward for everyone—including you and me."

He had a point, I had to admit it. The timing on this was way awful. If he and Spencer broke up right now, our winter break trip would be ruined. I could feel my resolve begin to crumble like the top of a cinnamon muffin from Le Petit Mitron. Crumbles: good for baked goods, less good for Mads's emotional stability.

"You know how I feel about you, right?" Tyler asked, stepping even closer, so near to me now that our noses almost touched. His eyelashes tickled my forehead. "Look—"

He paused, seeming to consider something. He looked at me, really *looked* at me.

And then he stopped talking for reals.

In a flash he had scooped a strong arm around my waist and swept me into the ladies' room, which was now, mercifully, empty.

He backed me into one of the marble-tiled stalls, closing the door behind us.

"Tyler!" My eyes flew open. "We can't do this."

"We *have* to do this," he insisted, lips pressing against my neck hungrily, hands exploring every inch of me. "I can't *not* do this."

I closed my eyes and whimpered slightly. This was wrong. I had promised myself I was going to be strong, that I wasn't going to settle, wasn't going to get with Tyler until things were over with him and Spencer for good . . . but with my fingers entwined in his hair, breathing in his fantastic woodsy-spicy boy smell, my mouth pressed against his . . . I literally could not help myself.

The ginger-champagne cocktails might also have had something to do with my capitulation. I'm willing to go out on that limb there.

Suddenly, the door squeaked and I heard a high-pitched giggle.

"Oh my *God,*" a voice announced, "Did she, like, mix Adderall and Xanax *again* or something? Because whatever the *hell* is going on out there is just embarrassing."

I didn't recognize the speaker, but I knew enough to keep absolutely silent. Tyler unraveled himself from our clutch and stepped lightly up so that his feet rested on top of the toilet seat. We listened, breathless, as whoever had come in made some fairly disgusting noises that I could only assume were related to major kissage.

Suddenly, the slurping stopped and a male voice said, "Babe, I'm not sure this is the best place for us."

It was *Dalton.*

Oh, God. This evening had just taken a turn for the even more messed up.

"What do you mean? We can be alone in here." Whoever the girl was, it definitely wasn't Regan. Spence would be disappointed.

I stayed frozen, worried that even a breath would give us

away. After what felt like several eternities, Dalton won out and our intruders finally left. As we heard the door swing shut behind them, we looked at each other and allowed ourselves to finally exhale.

"Do you think—," I began.

"Nah," Tyler said. "Definitely not. They were way too interested in each other to notice what was going on in here."

"Good," I said, quickly readjusting my shorts and patting my hair into place. I stepped out of the bathroom stall and glanced at my face in the mirror. My lips were puffy, swollen, but most of my friends would be buzzed enough at this point in the evening not to notice. Anyway, I could always write it off as a judicious application of DuWop Lip Venom—perfect for that Angelina Jolie bee-stung look. I glanced at Tyler and walked toward the door. "I'm going to make sure that the coast is clear, and once it is, we're going to get out of here." I peeked out.

"Right, cool, good plan," Tyler said, running his fingers through his hair. "And, hey, Madison? I just want you to know—"

"*Go,*" I whispered. "Now."

I was only being practical, of course—we needed to escape from our little illicit tryst while we were still unscathed and undiscovered. But there was a part of me that had another agenda as well. I didn't want to hear Tyler tell me again how much he feels for me, how he doesn't regret what we've been doing. Because as much as I feel the same way about him, of course, I can't pretend that I have no regrets.

I didn't stick around long after that. I was too twitchy and afraid that people (read: Spencer or Regan) would notice that something was up. Now I'm back home and safely tucked into my five-hundred-thread-count Egyptian cotton sheets. Maybe a good night's sleep will give me a new perspective on things. Hey, a girl can hope, can't she?

location: under cover
status: still Pop-Rocking
sleepwear by: Calvin Klein

Ty_It_On: is totally spinning, yo.

1 NEW RESPONSE TO "PLAYING YOU HOT AND COLD"

Toni_the_Tigress says: Merry Christmas, cats and kittens. Anyone too brain-dead (or blitzed) to be fully filled in on last night's scandal should feel free to e-mail me directly for details. Meow!

Prêt-à-Party

12/25, 10:16 a.m.
privacy setting: private collection

CURIOSITY KILLED THE CAT

Need. Info. Stat.

Somehow, I doubt Toni is referring to Kaylen's jumpsuit.

The Pop Rocks are back, and this time they're more like boulders. Oh, God. Oh, God. Oh, God.

How did she find out about Tyler and me? Apparently, someone actually did see us. Actually knew exactly what is going on. Actually went back out to the ball and told everyone what a raging skank I am.

Oh, God.

Oh, God.

Oh, God.

What if someone told Spencer? I just wish that she or Regan would return my calls.

Maybe they're still sleeping? Or enjoying their mounds of presents? It is Christmas morning, after all, even if it feels more like April Fools' Day to me.

I certainly won't be getting full enjoyment out of my many prezzies until I get some deets.

location: the Closet
status: what if?
worst fears: oh, God

Madison_Ave: is losing her freaking mind.

to: Madison_Ave@bradfordprep.com
cc: CaliforniaChic@bradfordprep.com
from: GoldenGirl@bradfordprep.com
date: 12/25, 12:08 p.m.
re: Where You at, Beyotch?

Mad Maddie—

Is everything okay? We lost you last night, and it's not like our prêt-à-partier to ditch out on a rager early! What gives? Hopefully, nothing serious.

Text or w/b/s so that we know all is well in Fashionistaland. I have three missed calls from you and my Spencer-senses are all tingly.

Muchos besos,

Spence (and Reegs)

to: Madison_Ave@bradfordprep.com
cc: GoldenGirl@bradfordprep.com
from: CaliforniaChic@bradfordprep.com
date: 12/25, 12:12 p.m.
re: Where You at, Beyotch?

What she said. Three missed calls each! We're worrisome worriers, with the worrying! Though I told Spencer that if anything were *drastically* wrong, like, life-or-death wrong, we'd have probably seen a Chanel-logo bat signal SOS somewhere out there in the night sky. You're probably buried so deep in couture gowns, dazzling jewelry, and fancy wrapping paper that you can't find your iPhone to respond.

We are contacting you back. Call us back-back pronto.

xx,

Regan

PS: When you skipped out early, you missed *all* of the fun—Trish Harlowe totes OD'd on a combination of Adderall, Xanax, and ginger-champagne cocktails and had to be rushed from the bash via stretcher. She's stable but humiliated. And apparently doesn't understand the dangers of mixing uppers and downers (and alcohol). Maybe she's headed for a stint at Zephyr (send our love to Paige, bitch!).

I think the pills were Mel's or Joanna's; they're both completely freaked that they might get busted for prescription drug abuse. How very Britney, yes? Tee hee.

Quel scandale!

to: GoldenGirl@bradfordprep.com,
CaliforniaChic@bradfordprep.com
from: Madison_Ave@bradfordprep.com
date: 12/25, 12:16 p.m.
re: Where You at, Beyotch?

Alive and mostly well, my friendlies. I think I must have had a bad oyster somewhere along the way last night. Raw bar = thematic (all that ice!) but potentially fraught with danger. I think Daddy's intense travel schedule may be negatively affecting his kitchens' quality levels (shh!).

Thanks for checking up on me. Love you, mean it (and you know that's the truth). Can't wait for our gift exchange.

Oh, and as for Trish Harlowe's mighty fall from grace: Holy Gabbana! I almost feel sorry for the poor girl.

Eh, waitaminute—no, I don't. Forget her.

Mwah!

Mads

Madison_Ave: is feeling much better now, thank you very much.

FilthyRich: might know something you don't know, but he ain't telling. Bros before hos and all that.

114

to: Madison_Ave@bradfordprep.com
from: FilthyRich@bradfordprep.com
date: 12/25, 2:56 p.m.
re: Best Joke EVER

Well, not really, but still . . . a majorly funny thing happened when I ducked into the ladies' room last night:

I was entering with a certain Tigress who was looking to play cat and mouse. But when I came up for air, I realized we weren't alone in our games.

I won't say anything—Tyler's my man, after all—and Toni has no idea. But you might want to play it cooler, going forward. I'm not sure Spencer would really be all that into a three-way. And some people aren't as discreet as I am.

Just a thought.

Peace out,

D

12/25, 3:03 p.m.
privacy setting: private collection

THE BRO CODE

While I definitely appreciate the aforementioned code for any number of reasons, the whole "bros before hos" thing leaves a certain unpleasant taste in my mouth. Because in the little Maddie-sensitive scenario as concocted by Dalton, if he and Tyler are the bros, well, that leaves me as . . . the ho.

Even worse: It's kind of hard to argue with that.

Let's just look at the facts, shall we?

Exhibit A, in four parts:

- slutting around behind closed doors

- behind people's backs

- with a guy who is, in fact, taken

- by my oldest and bestest friend

Also, we made out in a bathroom. *Cringe.* It kind of doesn't matter how classy and all that bathroom was. It's still a place where people go to pee.

I so can't take this anymore. I'm still a smitten kitten when it comes to Ty. I wouldn't be doing any of this if my feelings for him weren't real. But the stress and the guilt are ripping me up inside.

And the truth is that Tyler and I got sloppy. I mean, we *were* caught last night. The fact that Dalton doesn't plan to out us is sort of beside the point—anyone could have walked into that bathroom. Toni could have been more lucid when she wandered in, less interested in Dalton's lips and more in the prowling for gossip of the extra-juicy variety.

It could have been someone with less incentive to keep my secrets secret.

All I can say is, thank the Lord, Zac Posen, and Coco Chanel for Trish Harlowe and her journey to the valley of the dolls.

But what next? What am I going to do?

location: the Closet
self-loathing: acute
slut spiral: level 2, a.k.a. terror level yellow

GoldenGirl: Hey, lady. Merry Merry Christmas!

Madison_Ave: Thanks! Happy Christmas to you, too.

GoldenGirl: We need 2 talk.

Madison_Ave: ???

GoldenGirl: First off—glad you didn't, like, die or drop off the face of the earth or something last nite. We wuz concerned when you disappeared into thin air like that.

Madison_Ave: What can I say? I'm mysterious. I was mysteriously afflicted by a bad oyster. Which, well, I guess was especially extra mysterious becuz we all expect the best from Master Chef Takahashi.

GoldenGirl: OK . . . but here's the thing—and, you know, it's just us now. No Reegs around, much as I luv her. You and me: the original dynamic duo.

Madison_Ave: Again I say, ??? You're freaking me out a little, Spence.

GoldenGirl: So, yeah. I don't mean to be such a drama queen. But I have a confession to make.

Madison_Ave: Spill it.

GoldenGirl: I was, um, briefly concerned that the scandal Toni was posting about on her blog? Well . . . that it was . . .

Madison_Ave: SPILL!

GoldenGirl: That it was you.

Madison_Ave: Me? That's ridiculous. You were obviously over-reacting. You know? So your mind went to crazy places.

GoldenGirl: Hmm . . . You could be right. But something's been up with you. What's going on? Do you have a secret boy? Did you go back for seconds with that DJ?

Madison_Ave: No. Nary a dude. I am currently completely and entirely dudeless, despite recent brief kissage. You should know that! If there were someone, u'd be the first to know.

GoldenGirl: Well, yeah, that's what I assumed, but who knows? Like maybe it was a new thing, maybe you wanted to be all private about it, or maybe it was one of those things that is all sexy simply by virtue of being secret.

Madison_Ave: Sexy secret? You know all of my secrets. Sadly, none of them, at present, have anything to do with sex. I'm fine, really.

GoldenGirl: That's too bad. I was hoping there was some juicy gossip for you to share with me.

Madison_Ave: Well, I would, if I could. But since there isn't any . . .

GoldenGirl: Dudelessness. We need to remedy that. ASAP.

Madison_Ave: From your lips to Gabbana's ears, dearie.

GoldenGirl: Coolness. OK, must be off. I was thinking of doing a hydrating face mask before the big family dinner.

Madison_Ave: Kinerase?

GoldenGirl: Philosophy.

Madison_Ave: Ah. Enjoy!

GoldenGirl: Besos!

Madison_Ave: Mwah!

12/25, 3:43 p.m.
privacy setting: private collection

A CHRISTMAS LIST

Though perhaps not entirely true to the Christmas spirit, here is a list of the most spirited of contributions that the local shops have made to my Closet in recent days, unbeknownst to them:

- An art deco amethyst ring (5.7 carats, "vivid-deep clarity") not too terribly unlike the Tiffany cocktail ring that Tyler gave Spence after their last big blowup. And I didn't even have to put up with any boy-drama for mine. So there. Score one for the dudeless girl.

- A Burberry skinny cashmere check scarf that will look totes divine against my new:

- Prada royal calf clutch in sable. (Though this one seriously gave me a heart attack when I could have sworn the shopgirl glanced my way as I was stashing it under my coat. Paranoia runs deep.)

And that's not all! Behold:

- A jumbo bottle of Frédéric Fekkai Au Naturel Eco-Friendly

Styling Gel that I know Regan has been eyeing, the little greenie. It'll be a perfect stocking stuffer for her.

- A Guerlain limited-edition bottle of Shalimar Black Mystery perfume for Mom. (This is perhaps the acquisition of which I am most proud, in that it required the most elaborate subterfuge. There was a moment, just after casually scooping the box into my deliberately oversized ostrich-skin satchel, when the charmingly anorexic shopgirl called out to me from somewhere deep behind her counter. I seriously thought that she totes had my number. Naturally, I panicked, but I forced myself to remain calm. After all, darting off would only look that much more incriminating. Keeping my cool, I inquired about a trial set of lip treatment before strolling away. So, *phew.* And also, bonus: silky-smooth lips!)

I may have had a few close calls, but it must be said that I'm getting better at this.

And Mom does love the exotic florals of her gift, and with good reason. Constantly turning over, those scents are. Always something new and interesting with them.

Sort of like the most complicated and sophisticated of girlies.

Sort of like me.

location: the Closet, prepping for the traditional family
    Christmas dinner
status: bursting with elfin spirit and Christmas joy
fingers: Teflon-coated

12/25, 8:32 p.m.
privacy setting: ready-to-wear

DADDY KNOWS BEST

For reals, I mean. We may not have roasted any chestnuts in the fireplace at Casa Takahashi (very difficult to remove from the upholstery when they accidentally explode from the heat), but that doesn't mean that Dad wasn't fully inspired by the spirit of St. Nick. Despite all of his crazed busyness of late, he was able to pull it together to give us the classic Takahashi holiday treatment.

Christmas dinner was as per usual: just the three of us, in the formal dining room, menu by Daddy. First course was chilled oysters on the half shell, dressed in an aioli tartar, followed by a roast Christmas goose with basil pesto smashed red potatoes. Lest you think he copped out entirely by going the traditional route, we ate tapas around the fire before dinner was served. Oh, the things he can do with chestnuts, even with the restriction against open-flame roasting!

Despite the fact that none of us were actually hungry after the goose, we devoured a cheese course and then moved on to espresso and port back in the living room, in full view of the tree and all of our gloriously unwrapped prezzies. Dessert was a smorgasbord of pies, cakes, cookies, custards, and artisanal chocolate, which normally I would have been all over, but in this case, I was mildly distracted by gift-wrap carnage.

Mom drooled over her Shalimar perfume, and Dad actually teared up a bit to see his shiny sterling-silver flask. (Thanks for the inspiration, Spence!) I explained that it was for his many business trips, so that he could jet-set in style. He may have taken this as a tacit sign of approval for his increasing absences, which Mom might not have exactly loved, but . . . such is life. I also gave them a set of Murano glass wine bottle stoppers that I happen to know Mom had been eyeing at Saks. A good glass of vino at night seems to do wonders for their marriage, Dad's hectic schedule or no, so I felt extra proud of my Christmas-elf talents, even if Mom and Dad were oblivious to my subtle scheming.

As for me, I *completely* made out. Stocking stuffers included renewals of my *W*, *Vogue*, and *Elle* subscriptions and a shower of Chanel lip glosses and spa certificates. And then there was the mother lode: a set of hot-off-the-assembly-line high-end designing software . . . *and* a huge honking monitor to match.

Diane von Furstenberg has nothing on me. Or, at least, she should really watch her back.

I don't have to tell you that I am filled with the warm fuzzies. *Not* because of the ah-MAH-zing presents (although, yeah, those are nice), but rather, because in the wake of feeling mildly abandoned by dear old Dad and his exploding business—not to mention my own lack of boyfriendliness—it's nice to be all homey and cozy and loved, at least once in a while. Mom and Dad even seem moony and in love again. (It bears mentioning that Dad managed to stay off of the Crackberry for the *entire* Christmas Eve dinner. No small feat, that. It buzzed just the once, and the look on Mom's face was enough to make him tuck it away for the rest of the meal. I haven't seen it since. *Do not doubt the power of The Mom.*)

You ladies know that of the three of us, I'm hardly the sappy one. That's really Spencer's domain. But I'd be lying if I said I wasn't having major flashes of the sentimental today. Stick a bow on my head and sing me carols, I guess. There are worse things than going all Tiny Tim.

Drinks later with some oldies, friends of the 'rents. In the meantime, I'm going to savor being the anti-Scrooge.

location: fireplace-adjacent
status: so glowy you could barf
channeling: CindyLou Who

COMMENTS (1):
CaliforniaChic says: Can't wait to see what amazing things you design with your new kick-ass system, Mads!

GoldenGirl: will be breaking out the mistletoe—and fairy dust—later tonight!

to: Madison_Ave@bradfordprep.com,
CaliforniaChic@bradfordprep.com
from: GoldenGirl@bradfordprep.com
date: 12/25, 8:58 p.m.
re: Deck the Halls!

Hey, girlies:

I just wanted to check in while I'm on the way to my romantical dinner/gift swap with Tyler. We know how Mads made out, but did Santa do right by us all?

I have no complaints. Mother and Father managed to dig up a pair of emerald earrings worn by Grace Kelly to a *Vanity Fair* Oscars party back in the late forties. Something about a Christie's auction.

For her part, the brat seemed exquisitely happy with an autographed first-edition set of the complete Harry Potter series. Mind you, she's still too young to read. (She can be such a weirdo.) Or maybe she was just mesmerized by the private screening of *Babes in Toyland* that Mother and Father put together for her with some of her besties from playgroup.

Kyle couldn't be here for the holidays, unfortunately. Switzerland with his fraternity brothers. Next year we should *totes* arrange to visit. Cute college boys for my best friends!

And *speaking* of my best friends, we haven't set a time and place for our gift exchange. Wanna do a brunch tomorrow afternoon? We can rehash the family celebrations and sip brunchy drinks and generally keep up the tradition of being quietly and steadily hungover from now until New Year's Day.

What do you gals say?

Besos,
Spence

---

to: GoldenGirl@bradfordprep.com,
CaliforniaChic@bradfordprep.com
from: Madison_Ave@bradfordprep.com
date: 12/25, 9:12 p.m.
re: Deck the Halls!

Ooh, count me in. I've got good stuff for you both.

Have fun on your date, Spencer. (You sound so excited!
Cuteness!)

Mwah!

Mads

to: Madison_Ave@bradfordprep.com,
GoldenGirl@bradfordprep.com
from: CaliforniaChic@bradfordprep.com
date: 12/25, 9:28 p.m.
re: Deck the Halls!

Me three, me three!

Santa was *very* good to me this year: That YSL alligator bag
with the crystal clasp is mine, all mine. And there were some
fun little surprises inside the bag as well. Hee!

Shall we say noon tomorrow, Lacroix at The Rittenhouse?

xx,

Reegs

to: GoldenGirl@bradfordprep.com,
CaliforniaChic@bradfordprep.com
from: Madison_Ave@bradfordprep.com
date: 12/25, 9:32 p.m.
re: Lacroix

I'll take care of the reservation. Dad and Chef Lacroix studied together at Le Cordon Bleu once upon a time.

Laters!

WonderBoy: will be trying out his new SLR digital camera today, immediately, stat, pronto.

FilthyRich: got the massive multimedia entertainment system for his room that he was holding out for. Yeah, baby!

CatPower: thinks diamonds are a girl's best friend. And she should know now.

Toni_the_Tigress: is off to dinner wearing her new suede Fendi motorcycle jacket.

QweenKayleen: can't believe her parents managed to find an exact match to the Stella McCartney coat dress that Paige wore to her birthday party last year!

FrontPaige: took a mistletoe mud bath this morning. Fa la la la la.

12/26, 3:38 p.m.
privacy setting: private collection

BESTEST FRIENDLIES, BETTER SHOES

Can I make a case for brunch as the best meal of the day?

Come on, now—it's breakfast, it's lunch, it's savory, it's sweet, and there are even special drinks to go with! (I mean, can you even begin to contemplate a midnight mimosa? Negatory.) Brunch rocks. Especially when your company is of the veriest variety.

The presence of presents only made things that much more fabulosa.

We all arrived at noon sharp; we know better than to waste a favor called in by Dad. The restaurant was in full swing, brimming with Philly's finest. We were happy to be joining the well-heeled (and, frankly, knew that we were heeled with the best of them; we couldn't bear the thought of donning traditional Manolos or Choos in this particular venue, as both felt *mucho* derivative, but we did represent: Bottega Veneta, Chloé, and Moschino, respectively) and eager to exchange yuletide gossip.

Spencer said things had gone beyond well with Tyler during their dinner. She waggled her left-hand ring finger at us as she stabbed at her eggs Florentine. "It's so I can know that no matter what happens, I always have his heart," she said, indicating her Paloma Picasso for Tiffany Loving Heart ring in platinum with white diamonds. "Isn't it cute? It totally goes with those rose-gold earrings that I loved, which he *also* got me. *Aw*-ness. And actually, the shininess kind of matches the flask that I gave him."

I forced a bite of apple-cured venison sausage down my throat. "Did he like it?"

She nodded, flipping her long blond curls out of her eyes. "Ohmigod, he *loved* it. Said he's going to bring it to Aspen for clubbing and parties."

Of course he is. Tears sprung to my eyes, which I masked by coughing loudly and grabbing for my water glass. "Sorry," I sputtered after a deep gulp. "Sausage went down the wrong pipe."

Regan patted me on the back firmly and sighed. "Tyler always gets you the best jewelry."

"Well," Spencer replied, blushing lightly, "you can't go wrong with the little blue box." So true.

"Okay, okay, yayness and joy," Regan said, waving her fork. "We're so stoked that you and TyTy worked through all your differences and are feeling all lovey-dovey and in the holiday spirit and stuff. Really, really we are. But if I'm not mistaken, we have a gift exchange of our own to attend to, yes?"

I nodded, relieved that Regan had turned the conversation away from Spencer and Tyler. Not that I wasn't happy for my friend, of course, but why is it that lately, her happiness seems to come at the cost of a sharp, stabbing feeling in the back of my throat?

"I'll go first." Regan dove into her bag and rustled around for a beat or two before pulling out two identical envelopes adorned with glitter and bows. "One for you"—she handed an envelope to me—"and one for you," she said, passing the other to Spencer.

Spencer and I glanced at each other, then tore into our envelopes. We are not the types who need to be told twice.

"*Eee!*" Spencer shrieked, eliciting a dirty look or two from some of the restaurant's more genteel patrons. "Tickets to LA!"

"And a reservation for a bungalow at Chateau Marmont," Regan clarified. "For us, for the second weekend in March. We just have to remember to request a room that's far away from Sam Ronson, 'cause she always plays her music loud."

"Great minds think alike," I said, slamming my own two envelopes down in front of Spencer's and Regan's place settings. I'd added the Mad-tastic touch of sealing them with vintage brooches that I knew each of them would completely heart. "Read it and weep."

"South Beach?" Regan did a little happy dance in her chair. "Ohmigod, I have been *so* craving the mushroom risotto at the Delano! When are we going to South Beach?"

"Spring break," I said. "And you are welcome to indulge in risotto, but we're staying at the Mandarin on Key Biscayne. Dad's new restaurant there opens in April. So save some room for the signature Takahashi tartar."

"You guys, I can't believe it. How totally perfect for each other are we?" Spencer's baby blues threatened to spill over, and she dabbed at her eyes with the edge of her napkin. She sniffed delicately and slid one hand out from under the table, offering an envelope each to Regan and myself. She'd gone all out: satin ribbons, calligraphy, and confetti that sprayed across the table when we lifted our envelopes' lips.

My eyes bugged out. "Canyon Ranch?" I love, love, *love* the Ashiatsu barefoot massage therapy at Canyon Ranch.

Spencer practically burst out of her chair with excitement. "I was thinking after finals. But maybe we change our LA tickets so we can do a weekend in Tucson and then go on to LA from there? Take an extra-long long weekend?"

"I like the way you think," Regan said, downing the remnants of her virgin Bloody Mary. "Holy Santa Monica, do you girls realize what a supertastic year we have ahead of us? Aspen, South Beach, Canyon Ranch, and LA?"

"We are jet-setters," I said.

"We are *such* jet-setters!" Regan echoed. She glanced at her watch and frowned. "Unfortunately, I've got to cut this party short. The stepmonster is taking me for a pre-Aspen 'in-between trim.' She says that my layers are too long and I look like a disgrace." She wrinkled her nose. "But whatever, I'm adding on some aromatherapy after!"

"Just tune her out if she starts up," Spencer advised.

"Please. I'm wearing my iPod through the whole thing," Regan replied, cracking us up. She swept her bag up and kissed us both on the cheek before swanning out of the restaurant. I don't know how Regan can stand taking orders from a fake mother who's only a few years older than her. I couldn't handle it if my parents split up and Dad started dating a mere child. God, their marriage isn't that bad, is it?

The table felt much quieter in Regan's wake. I didn't know quite what to say to Spencer, whose new ring from Tyler shone like a beacon of my unrequited affections. I busied myself with my napkin.

Spencer leaned forward shyly. "To be honest, I'm kind of glad Regan left."

My eyes widened. Was she about to dish dirt on Regan? That wasn't like Spencer one bit. Spencer is all kinds of niceness personified.

"What up?" I asked.

"I got something just for the two of us," Spencer confessed, her words coming out in one breath. "You know, for old time's sake. BFF forever and all that. I got us facial massages at Cornelia Day Resort in New York City. I was thinking we could go one weekend while Regan is in LA visiting her mom, so she doesn't feel left out."

I must have looked unduly grateful, because Spencer peered at me. "What? Is that too mean? Do you think I should have included Regan? It's just . . . you're my oldest friend in the whole entire ever, Mads. I thought we should have something special, just the two of us."

"It's *fine*," I assured her. I contorted myself in my chair and fumbled underneath my seat, eventually resurfacing with a brightly wrapped box that I presented to Spence. I'd asked the maître d' to stash it for me before the three of us were seated. Mission accomplished. "For you. Please, to open."

She arched her eyebrows in delighted surprise, then tore at the box. Shredded paper flew everywhere, like happy, dainty detritus.

"Madison!" Spencer made a strangled sound that was completely undignified. I knew, then, that I'd done good. She jumped up out of her seat and threw her arms around me. "You designed this?"

I nodded, surveying her as she surveyed my latest creation.

It was a revised take on the classic LBD: Spencer, but with a daring twist. For starters, it was made of deep, smoky satin, dark enough, but not quite gunmetal, with an asymmetrical hem and a one-shouldered bodice that gathered and ruched at the waist. I knew it would perfectly compliment Spencer's willowy figure and cascading blond waves.

And I knew, based on the gleam in her eyes, that she adored it as I'd hoped she would.

"This is *fantastic*," Spencer gushed. "I'd wear it right out of the restaurant if I could, but that would be a total waste. It's going to be my New Year's Eve outfit."

I gasped. "Are you sure? New Year's Eve is a pivotal turning point, sartorially speaking. It kind of sets the tone for the rest of the year, you know."

"Which is exactly why I *should* wear it," Spencer proclaimed, causing my heart to do a funny floody thing that felt like I'd just chugged another mimosa when no one was looking.

But of course it was just bestiedom that I was drunk on.

I grabbed at Spencer's hand and gave it a squeeze. "The dress will look so good with your new ring from Tyler." Which, as much as it physically pained me to admit it, was completely true.

Spencer and Tyler are like the living embodiments of platinum and white diamonds: made to go together. Who am I to get in the way? I made my New Year's resolution right then and there: No more Mads and Tyler. Spence is my best friend and she deserves my loyalty. And yeah, so I've wavered a bit in the past, but it isn't going to happen again. I am all about the amends now, and the dress, not to mention everything it symbolizes, was the first step.

Spencer giggled. "I know. It's like you're psychic."

I smiled at her as widely as I could, taking some comfort in the fact that I was Doing the Right Thing. I decided at that moment that my superpower, such that it exists, has nothing to do with psychic ability and everything to do with self-sacrifice.

location: the Closet
Christmas joy: holding steadyish, for now
girlie weekends tentatively planned: a surfeit

12/26, 6:39 p.m., by Dalton Richmond

KISS MY ASPEN

Yo, party people:

Who-all is ready to get with the mile-high club?

That's right—Bradford Prep propers board the Boeing for parts west in two days. There'll be a major blowout on NYE—and no lack of other partying all week long.

I'll be packing plenty of protection.

(SPF of at least 15 for those mid-morning double black diamond runs. What? You thought I was talking about something else?)

See ya there. And if I don't, you weren't VIP enough to make the trip. Pity!

3 RESPONSES TO "KISS MY ASPEN"

Ty_It_On says: Yeah! Can't wait to find out who's been naughty (or if you plan on being *particularly* nice this winter break)!

CatPower says: TyTy, you know the holidays always bring out our most giving spirits. I'm sure you'll get plenty lucky. . . .

G-Money says: I've got an extra seat on my dad's G4 if someone needs to hitch. TM me.

12/26, 6:45 p.m.
privacy setting: ready-to-wear

SKI BUNNY CHIC

As if you friendlies needed my help in cleaning up nice! But still, for your reading pleasure, the fashion maven has compiled a short packing guide for our upcoming jaunt:

- two (2) velour tracksuit/extra-soft burnout tees/ballerina sneaker combos, one for the plane and one for downtime throughout the week

- one (1) snuggly-but-gorj pair of boots (I recommend Michael Kors Altitude, which are fur-lined and weatherproof but have four-inch heels)

- one (1) set of actual ski or snowboard attire, though fashion is always an issue (North Face will do, but Chanel, Louis Vuitton, and Celine are good designer options, as long as you can avoid the dreaded Inuit effect)

- one (1) drop-dead frock for the NYE bash to rival the annual Snowmass fireworks display + killer stilettos to match

- three (3) pairs of premium denim to encase the booty in a manner befitting so bodacious a body part, with corresponding cozy-but-sexy cashmere/angora/merino sweaters

- four (4) cocktail-style dresses of lesser impact than the NYE selection (but likewise hott) for any number of club nights throughout the week

- one (1) statement handbag; should be roomy enough for toting a designer dog.

- four (4) suitably slutty party tops

- one (1) party clutch too small to be practical but too gorj not to carry

- three (3) bikinis for hot-tubbing: skimpy, skimpier, skimpiest

And, girlfriends, don't forget to accessorize: jewels, hairpieces (tiara, anyone? It's *New Year's Eve*, for goodness' sake!), shadow liners, lip plumpers, illuminating powders, straightening serums, crimping irons, printed scarves, nail polishes (finger and toe), and exfoliating washes!

The key here? When in doubt: More is more.

location: fireplace-front
mood: still St. Nick-ly
wardrobe: cashmere drawstring pants and shawl-sweater

COMMENTS (7):

CaliforniaChic says: Can you believe it—three days and we're off in our own little winter wonderland. I can't wait! *Eek!*

GoldenGirl says: I'm just glad we get to ring in the new year together.

CaliforniaChic says: Me too! And, Mads—you and I are on a mission while we're away.

Madison_Ave says: ?

CaliforniaChic says: We've gotta find hotties to smooch on NYE @ midnight, of course!

Madison_Ave says: Of course. ☺ Ah, well, if all else fails, I'm happy to plant one on you.

CaliforniaChic says: Oh, please. Go for it! Then we'll totes have our pick of cuties lining up for us!

12/26, 11:45 p.m.
privacy setting: private collection

STOP THE PRESSES

Holy Gabbana!

And throw in some Chanel while you're at it. It's only proper.

Tyler came over this evening.

Of course, after my big epiphany at brunch and my resolution to rededicate myself to my friendship with Spencer, you can imagine my mondo shock at finding Tyler on my doorstep. I was mildly concerned at the idea that Mom or Dad would find the two of us—me barely clad and in animal print, at that—so I whisked him upstairs into the safe haven that is my bedroom.

"What are you doing here?" I asked, doing my best to sound standoffish, even as my heart did a little figure eight inside my rib cage.

He kicked his foot along the floor as color spread into his cheeks. Was it possible that Tyler was *nervous*? This was truly a Christmas miracle. I felt a little bolder; after all, I had a resolution to keep.

"What is it?" I prodded. "Seriously. We had a deal. No more sneaking around."

"You're the one who dragged me up here," he pointed out.

I wasn't letting him off the hook. "You're the one who popped up on my doorstep in the dead of night like some kind of raging, unhinged stalker-boy."

"Yeah, okay," he admitted, blushing more deeply. "I know that we—I know what I promised. But I still wanted to give you this."

Until now, I'd been so flummoxed by Tyler's drive-by that it hadn't even occurred to me to ask why he'd brought with him a duffel bag large enough for smuggling bodies. As he leaned forward to unzip the bag, my heart—and stomach—began an entirely new round of acrobatics.

"I got this for you. I have . . . I mean, my mom, you know, has a family friend who used to design for Valentino in France, so they were able—" He caught himself abruptly, thrusting a package into my hand. "Just open it."

I did, forcing myself to daintily remove the wrapping rather than tearing at the gift like a rabid poodle. My jaw dropped open. "Is this—"

Tyler beamed with pride. "It's an original."

"You got me an original sketch by Chanel. By *Coco Chanel.* You framed an original, signed copy of a Coco Chanel sketch. You imported it from Paris. For *me.*"

My insides summarily slithered into a buttery mess at the base of my stomach, leaving my resolutions and other good intentions coated in a slick layer of mush, gush, and sentimentality.

"For you," Tyler repeated softly. "But that's not all."

He reached back into the scarily bottomless duffel bag and pulled out something . . . something scarlet on a hanger . . . adorned with peacock feathers and Spanish lace.

I yelped. "The dress? From the sketch?"

Tyler nodded. "From the thirties, but well preserved. Save it for a special occasion."

I blinked, awestruck. Forget design software, forget a new monitor, forget even a girlie day at Cornelia Day Resort. This was the Best. Present. Ever. Tyler's gift to Spencer may have been lavish, but what he got me truly proved once and for all that not only does he care for me, but he also *gets* me, back and forth, inside and out.

Happy holidays, Coco Mad-emoiselle.

I decided to try the dress on for Tyler, right there in the closet, happily deeming the night to be a special enough occasion. He agreed.

And then I took it right off for him again.

location: bed
status: overwhelmed
chemise: lost somewhere, at some point, during all of the . . .
    gift giving

CatPower: is hitching a ride on the G4 with G-Money. Aspen, here we come!

12/28, 4:59 p.m.
privacy setting: private collection

THE FRIENDLY SKIES

The bulk of the Bradfordians arrived in Aspen this morning. A massive group headed off to the Sky Hotel to check in to various and sundry suites, but Spencer and Reegs and I are staying in Regan's mom's spectacular chalet just on the edge of town. We quickly dropped off our stuff, and after the grand tour (key stops: the enormo tented Jacuzzi, the great room, and the wet bar and fireplace in said great room, not to mention a private bed-and-bath suite for each of us), we changed into our ski clothes and headed out to the slopes.

And what slippery slopes they were.

When we arrived, Kaylen, Dalton, C.J., Toni, and Tyler were already camped out in the lodge, Kaylen clutching her cell phone and shrieking at some poor soul about ski equipment that had been damaged during her flight (I think she flew economy, bless her heart—no wonder). Spencer and Tyler clutched at each other and groped like they (a) hadn't just been all over each other during the entire cross-country flight and (b) weren't going to clearly be spending every single night in his deluxe king hotel suite anyway.

Like, jeez, folks—you've got a room. In fact, you've got two. Use them, for Prada's sake.

Tyler was cute enough to give me a Look upon arrival, though, and after his Christmas gift to me, the Look was all kinds of extra-specially loaded. I know he wanted me to understand that this trip is kind of a last hurrah for his relationship with Spence, to the point that even that grabby-grab was probably mostly for show. It's only a matter of time before we are all back home in Philadelphia, where Spencer will end up with Jeremy, Tyler will be with me, and we'll all soon be doing the whole happily-ever-after thing.

Sigh.

"So who's ready to get going?" I asked, clearing my throat loudly.

"Me, def," Regan said, tugging at her goggles, which hung around her neck. "I just need to grab my board and I'm ready to go."

"I'll ski with you," Spencer said. "If that's okay with Mads . . . because you'll be riding the chutes, right?" Of course, Spencer is a near-Olympic-level skier. And apparently, Regan's boarding skills are just as strong.

I pouted, trying to decide if I was really bothered by being abandoned by my friendlies. "Fine," I said. "I'll just head over to the bunny hill and ride up and down the Poma lift by myself all afternoon." I was joking, sort of. I was a strong enough skier before deciding that snowboarding might be more fun, once I get the hang of it. I'm better than the bunny hill. I'm just not black diamond better yet. But whatevs, our friendship totally transcends ski levels.

"I could—um, I could show you some snowboarding moves," Tyler chimed in.

I whirled to face him. Had he lost his ever-loving mind?

"That's a great idea!" Spencer exclaimed, clapping her hands together. "Regan and I will feel much better about going off into the wilds together if we know that you're in good hands, Mads."

Good hands. She was choosing to leave me in Tyler's good—no, make that *great*—hands. This was her decision.

What could I do?

I sighed, trying to look less distraught and less thrilled than I actually felt. "Fine," I said, as nonchalantly as I could muster. "Works for me."

After a quick round of hot chocolate with our peeps, we all split up and headed toward the mountain. (Except for Kaylen. She headed for the equipment rental. Ugh.) Once we were outside and out of sight from the others, I grabbed Tyler.

"Are you crazy?" I hissed. "We promised we weren't going to—"

"We did *not* promise that we weren't going to snowboard together," he insisted, cutting me off. "That is something that never came up."

I had to give him that one, however reluctantly. This scenario had definitely never entered my mind.

"Whatever," I retorted. "I mean, I have to go along with this now. If I don't, Spencer will definitely suspect that something is up. But we just . . ."

"We just what?" Tyler asked, eyes twinkling. Oh my God, was he actually *enjoying* my freaked-out frustration?

I think he was. *Grr.*

"We have to keep it together for as long as we're here in Aspen," I said. "There's just too much potential for us to get caught some-how while we're here, you know? It's too dangerous."

"Keep it together in Aspen?" Tyler feigned innocence.

"Yes. So you can teach me to snowboard or whatever, if you insist. It doesn't matter. Nothing is going to happen." Knowing that he and Spencer were definitely, for sure going to be splitsville once this trip was over made it easier to mean what I was saying vis-à-vis resolve.

"Well, one thing is going to happen," Tyler chirped, suddenly all playful and flirtier than ever.

"What?" I asked suspiciously.

"This." He lobbed a snowball at me lightly. It hit me square on the lift pass and dribbled down the front of my Chanel parka. I shook my head and brushed at the crumbles of snow with my gloved hand.

I arched an eyebrow toward Tyler. "You're on thin ice, my friend."

But then I giggled. I couldn't help it.

And so did he.

location: the great room
status: Schnapped
ice: ever thinner. Tyler + me + Spencer + Aspen = potential meltdown.

12/29, 3:01 p.m.
privacy setting: private collection

THE EARLY SNOWBIRD . . .

. . . *seriously* needs another latte. Like, immediately.

This is what I get for shacking up with a die-hard Cali-girl: Regan woke me at the crack of unholy *Christ* for a rousing session of Power Yogilates.

I shook my head at her, willing the sleep and confusion from my brain. "Wait, so is it yoga or Pilates?"

She flashed me a short Mona Lisa smile. "Yes." Well, okay, then.

Have I mentioned that I *despise* core strength training? To be perfectly honest, I'm not totally sure what my core even is. But try telling that to Malibu Perky.

What could I do? It was eight in the morning on my vacation; I didn't even have the words to argue with Regan about the many, many ways in which her idea of "fun" was deeply and inexcusably wrong. I just slipped on a pair of stretchy black drawstring flares, a sports bra, and a tank top.

"You'd better have hired us a car," I said, glaring at her. "No way am I *walking* to the exercise studio."

She blew me a kiss.

Ninety minutes and several contortions involving exercise balls of various sizes, shapes, and colors later, we were blissfully deposited back onto the streets of Aspen, our breath making cloudy patterns in the air as we chatted.

"That was intense," Regan said, rolling her head back and forth and rubbing her neck. "I need a mango-raspberry smoothie."

"That was *way* intense," I agreed. "Which is why I actually think we need Starbucks white chocolate lattes, size grande, and a Cranberry Bliss Bar."

It wasn't too difficult to twist her arm, and soon we were settled into a cozy table at the nearest 'Bucks (where she helped herself to a slice of lemon pound cake; girl has some slammin' genes, for reals).

"We can have smoothies later," I promised her, attacking my enormous frothy drink with gusto. "It's not an either/or thing."

"I'm so lucky I have you to explain how these things work," Regan joked, rolling her eyes. She picked a hunk of frosting off of the corner of her cake and popped it into her mouth. "Actually," she went on, reconsidering, "I *am* pretty glad you talked me into baked goodness."

I raised my eyebrows at her smugly.

"I can pay the favor back, you know," she said, suddenly all coy.

"You can buy me a package of cherry Twizzlers later and we'll call it even," I said.

"Or . . ." She paused for dramatic effect. "I could set you up with the majorly cute ski patrol guy that Spencer and I met while we were out yesterday. Tall, dark, kissable—*and* he's an athlete!"

I shrugged. I had no objections to tall, dark, or kissable, but it was hard to get too jazzed about someone I hadn't seen with my own two potentially more objective eyes.

"Come on!" Regan's mouth twitched into a wide grin. "Cute boy."

"Maybe," I said noncommittally. "I mean, are you even going to see him again?"

"We have his name: Cody Something."

"Cody Something. Very nice," I said sarcastically. "Of the Colorado Springs Somethings, I presume?"

147

Regan stuck her tongue out at me. "Please. How hard would it be to track down Cody's schedule from the ski patrol office? Maybe we'd even meet other hotties in the process."

"You're probably right," I said. I didn't feel like arguing with her and actually wasn't even really sure why I was being so resistant to any of this. Who am I to turn a blind eye to cuteness? Cuteness is good. We must seize the cuteness. I'm sure I saw that on a bumper sticker once somewhere.

"Or, I mean, there's always C.J.," Regan said. She deftly gathered her thick hair up and knotted it low and off of her face. "You guys get groiny sometimes, don't you?"

"Um, sure, and thank you for putting it so appealingly." C.J. and I have been known to make with the touchy-feely on occasion, sure. But what of it? WTF was she going on about, anyway? Was I suddenly some kind of charity case? I thought back to my IM convo with Spencer about me being terminally dudeless, and a cold, icky feeling came over me. My friends think I am hopeless. My friends think I am a freaksome guy-repellant who needs their help just to get smooched on New Year's Eve.

Blechness.

"I'm not desperate, you know," I said, feeling touchy. For a moment I almost spilled my secret; I mean, how much would it have shocked, I mean totally *floored* Regan to know that, in point of fact, I had been engaging in all sorts of smoochtastic behavior of late. With Tyler.

Obviously, I resisted the urge to blab. So I've made some iffy choices lately; that doesn't mean that I have a social death wish or anything like that.

"No, I know. *God,* of course, I know . . ." Regan's face turned purple and she glanced down at the table. "This is— okay, well, this is sort of embarrassing for me."

Embarrassing for *her*? What in holy Chanel was she talking about?

"Okay, here's the thing," Regan said, lowering her voice and moving closer to me. "Ryder's in town."

"Ryder *Jared*?" I couldn't help it; sometimes I'm crap at playing cool. Especially when there's good dirt involved. I knew that Regan and her rehab ex, he of indie film fest fame, still stayed in touch when they could. I *also* had a feeling that she might not be quite as over their relationship as she likes to pretend. The neon pink color crawling up her cheeks was total proof of that.

"Yes," she hissed, eyes darting around the shop. She'd already put in more than enough face time in the tabloids. "Anyway," she continued, taking a loud swallow of her café mocha, "he's having a thing at his chalet tonight."

"A thing? Like a party?" The appearance of this guy sure had Regan going in circles.

"Yes, a party thing. And—well, I want to go. I mean, it's been so long since I've seen Ryder in person. And he and I, we're totally cool, and we're just friends and all platonic and things these days, but—"

"But it's still a little complicated and you want a wing-woman at your side. So you were thinking, me and Cody, you and Ryder, and voilà."

"Yes, exactly." Regan sighed in relief. "And then we can leave Spencer and Tyler to do whatever it is that old married couples do. While we get our flirt on." I winced, which Regan mistook for hesitancy.

"I *swear* it will be fun. Rehabbed or not, I have it on good authority that Ryder still knows how to throw a rager. And, you know, forget about Cody Something, or C.J., or anyone else. We can meet new guys. *Vacation* guys. Resort-flingy guys." She tilted her head at me. "Or, you know, we can totally just do the girl bondage thing if you prefer. I just thought the idea of Y chromosomes might have more appeal."

"You thought right," I agreed. "I was—I was just being weird for a minute there. Sorry, I don't know what was going on in my brain. But, yeah, let's do it. You know I love to party. And it'll be nice to get outside of the Bradford bubble for a night."

"My sentiments exactly." Regan grinned.

"And who knows?" I mused. "A cute guy could be just what the doctor ordered."

It was a safer prescription than another dose of Tyler, anyway.

location: the Jacuzzi. *Mmm.*
status: bubbly
dudelessness: pending update

WonderBoy: is hammering with Habitat for Humanity and testing out his new camera south of the border. *¡Próspero Año Nuevo!*

12/30, 10:08 a.m.
privacy setting: private collection

THE BENEFITS OF YOGILATES . . .

. . . are really not to be underestimated.

Not that I'm about to start waking up early to exercise, like, every day or anything, but I can't deny that my BCBG burgundy toile hammered-satin halter top hung ever so perfectly off of my ultratoned shoulders at dinner last night. With my Rock & Republic gray skinny jeans and Louboutin ankle boots, I was ready for a fun meal with my friends . . . and then some.

In the end, it was the "then some" that got me into trouble.

We started the evening at Matsuhisa. My father had tipped me off that Chef Nobu was actually in the kitchen for the evening—an event as rare as a blue moon—so Daddy Dearest was able to snag us some VIP tables.

The VIP tables came complete with complimentary rounds of sake. Several rounds of sake. (Have I ever mentioned how much I heart sake?)

It was the usual suspects out for the evening: me, Spencer, Regan, Dalton, Tyler, C.J., and Kaylen. Camden, Toni, and Garrett had made reservations for a private dogsled ride to some restaurant just at the foot of Snowmass, so we agreed to check in with them later on in the evening. Unfortunately, by later on in the evening, some of us were out of commission.

After a few rounds of sake we were feeling livelier than ever, with Spencer feeding Tyler bites of spicy shrimp tempura straight off of her fork and Regan crossing her eyes at me from over the mini bonsai tree centered in the middle of the table.

For my part, I was happily chowing down on some black cod when Regan shrieked, then clapped a manicured hand over her mouth.

"What the hell?" I asked. "That was some kind of sonar you just emitted there. Unnecessary."

Regan laughed. "I just saw something. Or should I say, some*one*?" She stood up in her seat and beckoned off to one side. A moment later a figure appeared beside her at the table.

A tall, dark, and *kissable* figure, I should add.

"Madison," Regan called across the table. "This"—she waved her arm at Kissable—"is Cody . . ." She looked at him, prompting.

"Cody Parson," he said, filling in the blank.

"He works ski patrol," she told the table. "Why don't you sit with us?" she suggested, enunciating heavily. Her subtlety was most definitely on the fritz. She rose and flagged down a waiter, directing him to slide an extra chair into place next to me. "Cody has been dying to meet you ever since he heard about your mad fashion design skillz. No pun intended."

"Um, I don't know about *mad skillz*," I said, suddenly feeling an eensy bit shy. I didn't want him to think I was the second coming of Stella McCartney or anything like that. To thine own self be true and all. Boy really was kissable, I couldn't help but notice. "It's just, you know, something I do for myself."

"She's being weirdly modest. Ask her about the collection she has coming out this spring," Regan insisted.

"Really?" Cody's eyes widened. "That's cool. I've been looking into getting into modeling, you know?"

Tyler snorted from across the table. "Well, you won't be able to model her collection, unless you're looking to bring back the man-purse."

I shot Ty a look, then focused back on Cody. "Yeah, it's a line of bags that I'm doing for a local boutique."

"That's amazing!" Cody said, looking entirely undaunted by Tyler.

Fashion: the great equalizer.

Spencer and Regan might not have thought anything of Tyler's comment, but I knew Ty was being an ass because he was feeling jealous. Lovely. Well, Tyler could be as jealous as he wanted to tonight. He was there with Spencer, after all, practically eating right off of her plate. I'd been going to so much trouble pretending I wasn't noticing their happy-honeymooners routine that I was starting to give myself a migraine. Not ideal.

And suddenly I had Cody. So now Tyler wasn't the only one who was otherwise occupied.

Unfortunately, it took only about twenty-three minutes or so for me to realize that Cody was about as interesting as last year's Chaiken sweater coat.

"I think of myself as pretty Zen," he explained as I swigged at my sake like it was orange juice and I was coming down with the flu. "Like, I try to meditate every morning for at least an hour, you know, when I first get up."

I tried to keep my eyes from popping out of my skull. "I . . . did Yogilates this morning." Meditating for an hour sounded duller than a J.Crew catalog.

"Oh, sure, I mean, you gotta do that stuff, too, to ground you—but *after* the meditation. Like, you can't just skip one or the other."

"It was *Power* Yogilates," I protested, mainly thinking, *What the hell?* He was probably one of those people who preferred to sleep on a straw mat on the floor instead of a regular old mattress to, like, "ground himself" and whatnot. And he probably backpacked.

Backpacking always sounded so . . . *unsanitary* to me. Like, I think you have to *pay* to use the showers in some of those hostels and stuff.

"And I write in my journal at night, you know, mostly poetry. Like, to clear my thoughts before I go to bed."

"Mmm," I said, looking for a way out of the conversation. From the corner of my vision, I saw Tyler sling an arm around Spencer's shoulder. It temporarily strengthened my Cody-resolve. I reached my hand toward his.

"And I play bongos. To unwind."

I took my hand right back and slipped it into my lap. Bongos are a definite deal breaker.

It was a shame, really, seeing as how, from a purely aesthetic point of view, Cody remained as kissable as ever. But a girl has standards. I leaned back into the table, snapping my fingers in Regan's direction to get her attention.

"Hey!" I called.

She looked up from where it appeared she was having an intense, but lighthearted, conversation with Dalton. Hmm . . . more evidence of potential sparkage? I filed it away for future reference. "Hey, what?" she asked.

I gave the tiniest of head-bobs to show that I was basically over the Codemaster. On to plan B. I took another slurp of sake. "When are we hitting that party you were talking about?" I asked. I turned back to Cody, biting my lips in what I hoped was an apologetic gesture. "Sorry," I said. "It's a closed guest list. You understand."

[Sake monsters are doing a mambo in my brain right now. That's what VIP cocktails will do to you. I will brb after a healthy dose of Excedrin and VitaminWater.]

12/30, 10:34 a.m.
privacy setting: private collection

THE BENEFITS OF YOGILATES, PART TWO

Me again! All numbed from the pain and chock-full of watery vitamins! So where was I?

Right—anyway, if one was thinking that a party at Ryder Jared's Aspen hideaway would be not unlike a crazy eighties movie filled with Hollywood's idea of teens in over-the-top designer outfits and outsize accessories swilling froofy cocktails that no one in real life ever goes near, one would be one hundred and thirty percent dead-on. From the moment that we walked through the door, it was clear that Ryder's party was chaos, in the best possible sense of the word.

I do heart me some chaos from time to time. Especially when I've been in a love funk, as was threatening to overtake me this evening.

"I thought you said this was going to be a small thing," I called to Regan as she pushed her way through the throngs toward the kitchen, in search of our host.

She shrugged innocently, though through the crush, I could really only see the tips of her shoulders pop up and then quickly slide back down. I know Regan well enough by now to recognize a shrug by only the slightest muscle movement. The thought made me feel all loving and glowy.

Which makes me think the altitude was getting to me; I was twice as tipsy as I'd normally be after the amount of sake I'd had. I mean, I'd had a lot of drinks, but I was starting to feel more than a lot drunk. Way more than a lot.

Regan and I made our way through the kitchen to the hall-way, down a winding (and, frankly, given my state, treacherous) staircase, and into a game room. It was quieter downstairs, and less crowded, too. Ryder Jared and another guy were hunched over a foosball table, aggressively throwing themselves back and forth as each defended his territory.

"Hey!" Regan said, all chirpy and upbeat. She stood up straighter in her Free People tunic and tossed her hair off of her shoulders.

Ryder abandoned his post, leaving his opponent to thrust himself against the table one more time and scream, "Victory!" The thruster was summarily ignored.

"Regan! You made it!" Ryder broke into a wide, easy grin, one that I recognized from countless boy-detective movies from my early childhood and, more recently, from Portrait of the Artist as a Meth-Head. He looked just like he did on TV or in the tabloids. Except maybe a little bit shorter. And a *lot* less like a meth-head. Boy was *cute*. No wonder Regan had been all fluttery and flustered.

Ryder and Regan hugged, first tentative and awkward and then for real, squeezing each other for dear life.

"I'm so glad you came," Ryder said. His eyes were the color of the ocean just before a mondo rainstorm, and he looked like he meant it. "How have you been since the last time I talked to you?"

She laughed. "Keeping out of trouble." He arched an eyebrow at her. "Mainly. Oh, hey—," she said, sort of remembering me standing off to one side. (Seriously? Had I taken some sort of invisibility potion this evening?) "This is my friend Madison. She's from Philly."

"Hey, Madison," Ryder said, reaching over to give me a nonironic high five. "So you're from Regan's East Coast life."

"That's me," I said, smiling. "Coming at you from the City of Brotherly Love."

"That sounds so . . . friendly," Ryder teased.

"Yes, we're all with the warm and fuzzy," I confirmed. Regan impulsively squeezed me by way of demonstration.

When we got back upstairs, we discovered that the rest of our Bradford friendlies had arrived (Regan had decided more Bradford backup would help her gain the upper hand), and they'd gone ahead and made themselves comfortable on the leather sectional couch in the living room. Tyler and Dalton were rehashing their snowboarding exploits while Kaylen and Spencer pretended to care. All four of them sipped at tiny shot glasses of something, probably an after-dinner port. I knew that Tyler, especially, is fond of those, because nursing them late into the evening makes him feel mature and sophisticated. As if.

I shook out the negative thoughts. Hating on Tyler wasn't going to fix things, and neither was self-pity. Besides, what had he really done recently that was so terrible, anyway? So he was jealous of Cody for, like, three seconds back at dinner. I should have taken that as a compliment more than anything else. All of this drama was really messing with my self-confidence. My ego was starting to feel like a chewed-up piece of sugarless gum.

Dalton looked up as Regan, Ryder, and I hovered overhead. "Hey," he said, eyeing Ryder up and down. "Do you have any single malt?" I thought I might be picking up a tinge of jealousy from Dalton, which would certainly be a first. But he was probably just trying to figure out how this guy had managed to get with Regan while he was still hitting a brick wall.

"Of course, over there," Ryder replied, gesturing toward the wet bar. If he was daunted by Dalton's suaver-than-thou vibe, he didn't show it.

Single malt became double shots, which led to bottles of champagne. It didn't take long for us to kick back, sprawling drunkenly across the room. We gals were toasting away, deep in the midst of a round of "marry, screw, or kill," when a male catalog model leaned in.

"Which would I get?" he asked, leering at Spencer. Even from where I sat, I could smell the light beer on his breath. Grossness. "Why don't you screw me?"

"Leave it alone, man, and we'll leave you alone," Tyler said aggressively. He slid himself down the couch (one of the benefits of leather is that it definitely gives good slide) and wrapped a protective arm around Spencer's waist. "She's taken."

Spencer sighed. I could tell she was fed up with Tyler. She's always hated when he gets all possessive and stuff. Whereas for me, the idea of Tyler trying to publicly possess me sounds positively blissful, all issues of sexism aside.

Ugh. My ego had officially been downgraded to a chewed-up, *spit-out* piece of sugarless gum. I sincerely doubted it was possible to sink any lower.

But I was wrong.

"Jeez, no need to go all caveman, dude," said the catalog model, backing away with his hands up like he'd just been busted on a police drama.

"Really," Spencer said, shaking her head in frustration.

"Really," Tyler teased, bringing his fingers under her chin and pulling her in for a kiss. Despite her lingering annoyance, she melted right into him.

I know how she felt.

"What'd I miss?" It was C.J., back from a bathroom break and carrying a bottle of Jägermeister. The evenings always take a turn for the worse once the boys break out the Jäger. Tonight was to be no different.

"We were playing a game," Kaylen said. "You know, marry, screw, or kill. You just—"

"I know the rules," C.J. said, cutting her off. "You pick

three people and decide: which would you marry, which would you screw, and which would you kill?"

"And no passing or skipping turns," I informed him.

"Wouldn't dream of it," he said, giving me a heavy-lidded grin.

I didn't mind it, truth be told. I didn't mind being eyed by *someone,* even if it wasn't the someone that deep down I truly wanted. I didn't mind it one bit.

"What would you pick for me?" he asked. He took a long sip from the bottle he still clutched. I could smell the alcohol as he swigged. It was fiery and thick, and I wanted to taste it for myself.

"For you? Um, it depends on the two other people." I was stalling for time.

"Me, Dalton, and Tyler," he offered.

Huh. Well, that *was* an interesting question. I paused for a moment, thoughtful. "Okay," I said finally. "I've got it: I'd marry Dalton—and then divorce him for all his money."

Dalton laughed. "It's called a prenup, baby."

I ignored him. "And I guess I'd have to kill Tyler." If Tyler overheard me, he didn't respond.

"So . . . what about me?" C.J. asked, his tone suggestive.

I was starting to see a light at the end of the Longest, Most Single-est Night Ever. There was one way to answer that question, to inhale the fire, and to do something proactive about the wadded-up gum feeling all at once. It involved throwing myself at C.J. and totally going for it in a most unladylike manner. Which I proceeded to do. No holds barred.

I didn't even realize how horizontal we'd gotten or for how long until I felt slender fingers on my shoulders pulling me back. When I sat up, the room was spinny and unfocused. C.J. looked as dazed as I felt. His shirt was unbuttoned—Who had unbuttoned his shirt? When had that happened?—and his faced was smeared with lip gloss that looked suspiciously similar to my Dior Addict shine glaze.

"I don't—," I started, but before I could complete the thought, Spencer had yanked me to my feet and pulled me toward the kitchen. A glass of water was thrust into my hand, and she ordered me to drink.

"What the hell was that?" Spencer's eyes flashed with concern.

"What do you mean?" I asked. The glowy effects of the sake and champagne were starting to wear off, and now everything just seemed dull and filmy, like I was dog-paddling through mud.

"Madison. You were practically getting naked with C.J. on the floor of Ryder Jared's house."

"So? C.J. and I have hooked up plenty of times." The girl who was speaking didn't even sound like me. She could barely form coherent sentences. And the room was really tilting off to one side at the moment.

"Okay, fine, but usually you're actually behind closed doors when that's going on, not starting to remove each other's clothes right in front of us," she said. "Or do you have some secret, weird, kinky fantasy of putting on a show for a roomful of people?"

I couldn't quite make out the tone of Spencer's voice. It was more than fury, more than bewilderment. She sounded almost . . . urgent.

"Spence, I'm sorry. You're right. I wasn't thinking. But why are you so upset? What do you care if I make out with C.J.?"

"I *don't* care if you make out with C.J.," Spencer insisted. "And honestly, I wouldn't care if you wanted to strip down naked and give that Sears model a lap dance, if I thought it was a conscious choice that you were making. But getting plastered and getting it on in front of half of our friends really isn't like you, Mads. Or it's not like the old you. So I thought maybe I should step in."

"You should. I mean, you did. And . . ." I paused. "Why is the room so spinny?"

"Okay," Spencer said. "That settles it. First water. Then home. Then more water."

I agreed, in that I didn't really have the energy (or the ability) to disagree. We left.

I drank the water and it helped a little—but I still had a nagging feeling in the pit of my stomach. Not about what I had done, but more about what Spencer had *said*, about how making out publicly with C.J. wasn't "like me."

She was right, of course. It's not like me at all.

What *is* more like me? Making out privately. With *her* boyfriend.

And just when I thought I couldn't feel any crappier about myself.

location: bed, still
status: hungover, still
self-esteem: plummeting, still

Madison_Ave: Where have u been, Ty? U haven't written back to any of my texts.

Madison_Ave: Is this because of last night? Cuz u knew that C.J. and I hook up sometimes. Besides, you had Spencer. You HAVE Spencer. U really have no right to be jealous.

Madison_Ave: Right. OK. Whatever. Well, call me or text me back if you decide that you want to talk.

———————————

Ty_It_On: can't handle that, man.

12/30, 2:43 p.m.
privacy setting: private collection

THE LONELIEST NUMBER

No Regan. She's back on the slopes, and I couldn't bear to join her, especially not in my current state of hungoverness. She also denied all of my suspicions having to do with any lingering feelings she may still have for Ryder Jared. Methinks she doth protest too much. Kind of like how she keeps insisting there's no underlying chemistry between her and Dalton. (I, for one, am starting to think that maybe Spence was right about that.) Or maybe Regan's true feelings for Ryder complicate the sparkage with Dalton.

No Spencer, either. She and Tyler are backcountry skiing for the morning, and three would definitely be a crowd.

Emphatically no C.J. I think we both need some time to gear up for the ragingly awkward tension that's sure to blossom the next time we're both in the same room.

And no Kaylen. Just . . . no.

Which leaves me with . . . well, not very much.

Good thing I'm still feeling roller coasters streak across my frontal lobes. I'd be lousy company right now anyway.

location: bed. The room is steady once again. It's delightful.
status: see above re: steadiness and delight
self-esteem: bottomed-out? Here's hoping, anyway.

12/30, 6:02 p.m.
privacy setting: private collection

GETTING MY ROCKS OFF

And rock-bottoming-out. For real this time.

I honestly had no idea it was even possible to sink any lower. Pretty soon I'm going to need to wear a scuba outfit just to leave the house.

Honestly, all I meant to do was a little window-shopping this afternoon. Get out of the house and avoid the crew when they came back from skiing. Maybe pick up a new eyeliner or something, anything to perk me up and out of my recent funk. I don't even know how to explain what's been going on with me.

The thing is, I don't go into a store with the plan to swipe something. Thanks to Daddy's little empire, I can totally pay for whatever I need, or even whatever I want. It's not about money, and usually, it's not about whatever the thing in question even is. It's about . . . it's about that buzzy feeling in the back of my throat when I see something, on a shelf, on a table, in a display. Something that beckons to me from across the store. Something that I know that someone else would covet. Before I can even clear my head, that little buzz spreads like an electric current, through my scalp, down my arms, and into my belly, and then it's like adrenaline just takes over. I'm just a flash of red, of energy, and before I know it, my hands have wrapped around whatever thing I'm reacting to and then . . . it's mine.

And no one knows.

It's powerful, that sensation, and considering I've been feeling kind of powerless in other aspects of my life of late, it's addictively refreshing.

And even if that thing then sits in my dresser drawer for

the equivalent of a light-year, *I* know it's there, and that flu-ish, feverish sensation stays with me. For a while, at least.

That's how it's *supposed* to go, anyway.

But that's not how it happened today.

Today everything fell apart.

It was my fault. I was sloppy. I should never have gone out as exhausted and drained as I was. I should have stuck to the original plan, the window-shopping plan. I should have *paid* for the pashmina. I should have kept a closer eye on the salesclerk. I should have noticed her keeping a closer eye on me. I should have dropped the whole thing, walked away from the crime, the store, the pathetic-ness of my sad little-girl-lost routine, the minute I caught her eyeing me.

Should, should, should.

It's easy enough to pinpoint what went wrong, now.

Anyway, there I was, blood pounding in my temples, urging me on, while tiny drumbeats in my belly told me, *No, don't do it, this is the wrong time, the wrong place.*

I did it anyway.

And no sooner had my hands wrapped around the pashmina and slid it into my Louis Vuitton bucket bag than she was on me.

"Miss, I'm sorry, but you'll have to come with me."

I spun, my jaw dropping open. "I—"

The salesclerk, all frosted highlights and liquid liner, wasn't interested in my protests. "We've got you on the security camera," she said. "You're going to have to empty out your bag."

I looked right and left furtively, wondering if anyone in the store knew me, was seeing this, was going to report back to my friends or—oh, God—my parents. My eyes filled with tears as she escorted me into the back office.

I dutifully handed over the bucket bag, frantically gnawing at one fingernail while she pawed through it, triumphantly retrieving the scarf.

"You know our policy," she said, her voice thin and brittle.

I shook my head.

"We prosecute shoplifters."

Bile rose in the back of my throat. No *way* would my father tolerate that. "Please—I can pay for it."

"Then you really should have."

Touché.

"Can I—can I at least make a phone call?" People in jail get one phone call, don't they? I know that from endless *Law & Order* episodes. So maybe I wasn't technically in jail—yet—but this was the closest I'd ever been, and I wasn't looking to correct the technicality.

She sighed and blinked her heavily shadowed eyelids. "I suppose. You stay here. I'm going to call the storeowner. We'll see how she wants to handle this. And if you're tempted to leave, keep in mind that we have a security guard posted at the entrance to the store."

I swore to her that I wouldn't leave, and she ran off to locate the storeowner as she'd threatened. I sat perfectly still on my tiny plastic folding chair and wondered who, exactly, I thought I was going to call. Who I thought could help me right now.

Spencer was the obvious choice, seeing as how she's my oldest and closest friend. But Spencer's the favored daughter, the queen bee, the Golden Girl, and I couldn't bear the thought of revealing my ugly secret to her, especially after her little lecture last night. Regan probably would have understood, since she'd been through a similar embarrassment with rehab and everything, but I didn't know if I totally trusted her not to say anything to Spencer. Why did it all have to be so complicated?

I scrolled through my phone book. *Tyler.*

Could I call him?

Did I dare?

What would he think of me? I really didn't know, but I really didn't have a choice, either. I tapped at his number.

It felt like six hours passed before Tyler showed up, though I'm sure in reality it was more like thirty minutes. He did not seem amused by my predicament.

In fact, the only person in the entire store who was maybe more pissed off at me than Tyler was the storeowner, who arrived just after Tyler and whose elbows were so sharp, I feared she'd slice me open with one rogue gesture. *She* wanted to throw the book at me. (What book? But isn't that what they say? Probably a heavy one, at any rate—if Owner Lady could even lift anything thicker than a Mad Libs.)

"Be reasonable," Tyler said, hooking his index fingers into the pockets of his jeans. I had to admit, he looked plenty reasonable himself. I couldn't believe this woman wasn't jumping on board with him.

"Store policy is store policy," she said. I worried for her; if she grimaced any wider, her eyebrows were going to pop off.

"I'm sure you can make an exception for a Takahashi," Tyler said.

The owner's eyes flew open, and I wondered why it hadn't occurred to me to use my name before. "Wait, she's . . . Mr. Takahashi's daughter?" Everyone knows my father, especially in a resort town like Aspen. Clearly, the trauma had interfered with my normal brain functioning. Could I be blamed for not thinking straight?

Tyler realized he was halfway toward reeling her in. He softened his gaze, stepped closer to her. "How about this: You let her go, and we buy the scarf from you, plus a few additional items . . . and this woman here"—he indicated the salesclerk who'd busted me—"gets to keep the commission."

Salesclerk swallowed visibly. I could tell that she liked that idea.

"A sale is a sale, right? And this way, you don't have to alienate a man who is *extremely* friendly with the head of the local zoning board," Tyler pressed.

The owner tapped her fingers against the surface of her desk, apparently considering. I could tell she wanted to take Tyler up on his suggestion, but she didn't want to appear to cave too quickly. Still, though, my nerves were a bundle of barbed wire.

"Okay, just this once. And on the condition that she"—the owner shot me a nasty look—"doesn't shop here again."

I nodded meekly. As it was, I wasn't sure I'd be able to set foot in this town again, much less in this store.

Tyler halfheartedly grabbed a few things off of the main floor; I didn't even bother to see what he was picking out. What did it matter? Once he was done, I slid out my platinum card and paid for it all, feeling like a slithery, slimy fraud as the clerk folded everything neatly in a glossy shopping bag.

"Have a great day," she smirked, passing my packages toward me over the counter.

"I will," I mumbled as Tyler led the way out of the store.

He didn't hold the door for me or look back at me as we strode toward his rental car. He didn't say a word on the drive back to Regan's either.

Not that I blamed him. What was there to say, anyway?

location: bed. I've decided I'm never coming out again.
  Nothing good ever comes of it anyway.
status: Aspen's most wanted
purchases: languishing on the floor. Do I even know anyone
  who still wears pashmina? Oh, well. Maybe I can give
  the scarf to charity or something. That's me. Filled with
  charitable intentions.

QweenKayleen: has her hairstylist and makeup artist on speed dial for tonight.

---

1 NEW RESPONSE TO "KISS MY ASPEN"

Toni_the_Tigress says: Talk about ringing in the new year! This bash was a blowout, with some friendships—and relationships—blowing *up*! Have I mentioned how much I love New Year's Eve—and drama?

1/1, 5:22 a.m.
privacy setting: private collection

DOWN FOR THE COUNT

If January is a chance for resolutions and new beginnings, then I'm in.

I've got nowhere to go but up.

But that's probably easier said than done. *Way* easier said than done.

It's not as though New Year's Eve didn't start out on the right foot. Spencer had arranged a sleigh ride to a mountaintop restaurant for dinner, and she'd even booked us a private banquet room where we could get silly all on our own. I mean, not that we ever need an excess of privacy in order to let the good times roll.

We had our own wait staff, a classic menu, and enough Veuve Clicquot Rosé to bathe in. We girlies were stylin': me in the special Coco Chanel (from Tyler, but he and I were the only ones who knew that, and I doubt that he was spilling), Spencer in the dress that I'd made her, and Regan in an amazing vintage I. Magnin white crepe cocktail number. She matched the snow flurries that had begun to fall outside. It was almost a shame to have to bundle up in our shearlings on the way there in an effort to keep out the chill.

I toasted, blabbed, and laughed so much that by the end of dinner, my stomach hurt from too much of a good thing. But we were just getting started; there was way more to come.

Regan had told us that she'd take care of getting her house party-ready, and by the time dinner was over and we'd made our way back, we realized just what, exactly, her little elves had been up to.

The entire great room was lined in soft candles, and the fireplace glowed (which was nice, considering our skimpy attire). Uniformed servers moved swiftly through the space, passing out canapés and champagne, ready to offer up anything that wasn't immediately visible to the naked eye. Fragrant jasmine crept along the banisters, and out on the oversize deck a band had set up inside a heated tent and was already jamming as we arrived.

Regan had done good. Really, *really* good. No matter how lousy my vacation had been up until now, I had renewed faith in the power of New Year's Eve.

I watched everyone's eyes light up as they entered the

house one by one. Spencer even let out a tiny gasp of surprise. Dalton grabbed Regan into a one-armed hug.

"This is awesome," he said. "You really know how to throw a party."

"Did you doubt me for a second?" she asked.

He put his hand to his heart. "Not for one nanosecond. Scout's honor."

She shot him a look. "Why do I have a feeling that you were never a Boy Scout?"

"My mother is a Sister of the Main Line—don't I get credit for her philanthropy?"

To *her* credit, Regan only laughed. "Get yourself a drink and head outside. The band is already halfway through their first set, and they're amazing. They were recommended to me by—"

"By me." Ryder Jared stepped forward and kissed Regan on the cheeks in a Hollywood hello. She looked rather pleased to see him. Dalton, less so.

For a while everything went along the way parties are supposed to: Some hair got mussed, some glassware was broken, and I may or may not have seen a scalloped La Perla balconette bra swinging from a Tiffany stained-glass lamp. But, hey—it's not a New Year's Eve party if there isn't some lingerie getting loosened here and there, right? Still, as the little hand crept ever closer to twelve, I felt the first stirrings of pure panic fluttering in my rib cage.

Midnight loomed. And me, all by my lonesome, with no one to mack with.

I wandered from the kitchen into the great room to see what people were up to. They seemed to mainly be up to each other, as in pairing off with, before the proverbial ball dropped. One couple stood out from the crowd: Tyler and Spencer, obvs, draped across each other in that way that only long-term twosomes have about them, sipping wine out of the same

Waterford glass and giggling quietly to each other. They were clearly down for the count and settled in for the night, and probably not looking for a threesome.

(Disturbing thought. Ickness. Is there any way to rewind my own brain?)

"You guys!" A more sober, more alert me would have jumped at the high-pitched sound. It was barely human; it was Kaylen. She'd crawled to the top of a table—I winced, watching her four-inch mules scrape against the polished mahogany—and was doing a sort of impromptu shimmy.

She flipped forward and back upright again, grabbing the skirt of her dress up with her. Needless to say, she was going commando. She'd pulled a full-on young Hollywood.

Unnecessary. *Highly* unnecessary. *Yech.*

"Holy Ga—" I turned, only to realize there was no one beside me to turn *toward.*

Sadness.

"You *guys!*" No one seemed especially fazed by Kaylen's rather . . . ahem . . . *naked* display, but that didn't deter her. "The countdown is starting!"

This announcement was met by general hooting, hollering, and catcalling. The evening had definitely begun to deteriorate, skidding downhill at an alarming rate.

With her skirt back where God meant it to be, Kaylen took charge of the backward counting thing. Which, given how utterly plastered she was, was kind of impressive. I'm not totally sure I would have expected her to be able to count backward from ten when sober, so, you know . . . I had to give her some credit.

"TEN!"

I glanced back across the room. Spencer was perched on Tyler's lap and her hands were wrapped around his neck. They were doing the whole gazing-intently-into-each-other's-eyes thing that you always see in barfy movies or cheesy TV shows.

"NINE!"

C.J. stood in the corner of the dining room drinking Veuve straight from the bottle. After a particularly hearty swig, he ran the back of his hand across his mouth. He looked up and caught my eye, flushed, and then turned away again. Yeah. That was awkward. We still hadn't quite lived down our peep show of the other night. And we were most definitely *not* going to do a repeat of it this evening. Countdown or no.

"EIGHT!"

Dalton sidled up next to me. He looked straight at me and mouthed along with Kaylen, *"Seven. Six. Five."*

Please, Lord and Christian Dior, no. It hadn't come to that. The boy had been with Paige, Cam, Toni, and maybe even Regan, just within the past month or so. Sloppy seconds is bad enough, but fifths? No, thanks. I don't care how cute he is.

At that point in the night, I still believed that I could preserve whatever tiny shred of dignity still existed somewhere deep in my core.

Ha.

Dalton placed a firm hand on my hip. *"Four. Three."*

I swatted his hand off of me, slipped away from him, and ran for the last place I'd seen Regan—the deck. She'd been flirting with one of the band members, the one with the map of Newark, New Jersey, tattooed on the underside of his wrist.

We were soul sisters, Regan and I. Partners in singledom. Maybe we'd make Newark's night and each smooch him on one cheek when the ball dropped. Or maybe we'd make his year and kiss each other. (Please. It would be totally chaste and PG.) At the very least, I could hug my girl. That's what single friendlies do on New Year's Eve.

"TWO!"

I stopped in front of the balcony, blinking to be sure of what I saw through the sliding glass doors. It was Regan. Mid-smooch. And while she wasn't entwined with Newark, she *was* pretty much glued to the front of Ryder Jared. They both had their eyes closed. No way were they going to notice me, no matter how long I stood there doing my best poor Little Match Girl. And I was feeling kind of pervy for checking them out through the door.

No lingering feelings, my (extremely cute, extremely perky) ass.

"ONE!"

So that was it. My New Year's. My single, solitary New Year's. No boyfriend, no hookup, no holiday fling. Not even a girlfriend to squeal with and tell each other how pretty we are.

"HAPPY NEW YEAR!"

Happy New Year, I told myself. *You're very, very pretty and your dress is bangin', too.*

Somebody had to say it. Anyway, a healthy self-image is important for a girl my age.

And many fan-freaking-tastic returns.

I wish I could say that the night had ended with the countdown, with the ball dropping and Kaylen's skirt lifting and every single other person on the face of the planet kissing another living being while I stood by, clutching a champagne flute with a smile glued onto my face.

That ending? Option A? Well, it would have been depressing as hell, yeah, but I could have made it work. Because in that option, at least, even if my friends were, um, busy getting busy at the stroke of midnight? At least in that scenario, as that reality played out, they remained, now and forever, my friends.

If only.

Spencers are forever, I said. That was, like, the Golden Girl rule?

Well, they say rules are meant to be broken. It's something we Bradford Prepsters know better than anyone.

It's something *I* know better than anyone.

Too bad there's no one around I can talk to about any of this.

Seeing as how none of my friends are talking to me.

Especially not my Spencer.

location: do you really have to ask?
head: pounding
guilt: suffocating

Toni_the_Tigress: totally effing called it, did she not?

FilthyRich: can't believe someone managed to out-scandal the major hookup session between Regan Stanford and that Hollywood has-been last night. Wow.

CaliforniaChic: did not see this one coming.

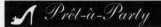

1/1, 8:12 a.m.
privacy setting: private collection

OMFG NYE

So here's what happened:

The upside to being alone for the kissfest at the stroke of midnight on New Year's Eve? Once everyone pairs off and starts with the gropealicious behavior, it's easy to sneak out unnoticed. I could have jetted off to Peru and I don't think one person would have looked up from his or her location at Château Stanford.

Not that I blame them. I just felt a touch, well, invisible.

Little did I know at the time that invisibility would have been a *major* asset to me, all things considered. Given what was to come.

When Kaylen began krumping on the dining room table, I decided my voyeurism had hit a point of diminishing returns. I rubbed at my eyes to remove the vision of her lady-bits from my brain, then wandered outside to the lower level of the deck. The Jacuzzi area was also covered with a transparent tent, which made it a serene, isolated space from which to watch the snowfall. I actually couldn't believe that it hadn't been overrun by hormonal couples, but I guess they were too busy inside, closer to the alcohol and the other creature comforts. It was chillier down here but not unbearable. Regan had obvs done some major investing in heat lamps.

I took off my shoes and dipped my feet into the water, careful to keep my precious dress far away from chlorine and other chemical badness. It was warm, and as it bubbled up around my shins, I allowed myself to relax, to let go of the pressure that had been building up inside of me since we arrived in Aspen. So it was New Year's. So what? Who cared that I hadn't kissed anyone when the clock struck twelve? It wasn't like I *couldn't* have kissed someone if I'd wanted to. Dalton may not have been my first choice (or especially choosy himself), but he's a hottie, and he wanted me. And he wasn't the only boy at that party. I was just taking a break from guys.

Yeah, that was it. After everything that had gone down with Tyler, maybe I just needed some space. Some time to clear my head. And hooking up is the exact opposite of head-clearing behavior.

I took a deep breath. Head-clearing, cleansing, soul-scrubbing behavior. That was what it meant, ringing in the new year on my own. Atoning for the bad decisionitis of previous months. Vowing not to repeat said bad decisions. I felt righteous, resolved. Like a fresh snowfall. Completely unblemished.

Looking back, it's clear that I was just asking for trouble.

"What are you doing out here in the snow?"

It had been so quiet out on the deck, I'd almost forgotten that there was an entire party—sixty or so of my closest friends—inside the house all this time. But here was Tyler to remind me.

"It's not snowing on the hot tub," I pointed out.

"Isn't it technically a Jacuzzi?" he asked.

I splashed at the water with my big toe. "What's the difference?" Even though I knew. A Jacuzzi has the jets. "Where's Spencer?"

"Inside. She passed out almost immediately after the ball dropped." He shrugged, settling himself next to me. He took his shoes off and rolled up his pants, joining me in dangling his feet in the tub. "Everyone did. It's like a morgue."

"Nice image."

"You know what I mean. Prone bodies all over the place."

It was my turn to grin. "Regan will be so pleased with the way the evening went."

"Yeah, it was a good party," Tyler agreed. When I didn't reply immediately, he glanced at me. "Don't you think?"

"Um, yeah." He knew better than to prod about this, right? I mean, he *had* to. I know that boys aren't always the most ultrasensitive, but still.

"I'm sorry," he said suddenly, placing a hand on my knee. His voice was urgent. "I didn't mean to be such an ass the past few days."

"Yeah?" It was an easy enough claim to make, with his girlfriend unconscious an entire floor above us.

"Yeah. I just . . . I know we're not supposed to be together yet, at least not until I can end things with Spencer the right way, and I think the new year is going to be a good time for new beginnings for us—"

"Definitely."

"But I won't pretend it didn't piss me off to see you going at it with C.J."

I made a face at him. "Come on."

"No, really. Look, I know you've hooked up with him plenty of times in the past—and that I have no leg to stand on when it comes to this stuff—but do you think that makes it easier?"

I softened, Gabbana help me. He was being so sweet. And I was feeling so lonely. And the water was so warm. I am not made of stone. "And what about yesterday? When you . . . came to help me out?"

"With the . . . thing?" Apparently he's unable to even utter the word "shoplifting" out loud. Which was just fine by me. I didn't really want to face the reality of my dirty little habit. "Well, Madison—can you blame me? You freaked me out! Maybe you're not my girlfriend, maybe we're not, like, *together*, but you scared me. I don't like to see you getting yourself into situations like that."

I felt a splash of wetness on my cheek and was surprised to discover that I was crying. "Me neither," I admitted quietly. "But sometimes I can't help myself." I looked up at him. "What's wrong with me?"

He shifted closer to me, his legs dragging ripples in the surface of the water. "God, Madison, nothing is *wrong* with you. Look, I'm sorry, I didn't mean to upset you. I just wanted—I just wanted to be honest with you, so that maybe things could go back to being normal between us."

I chuckled. It was a short, bitter sound. "Normal? Like back when we were just friends, running around pretending there wasn't any attraction between us? I don't know that things ever were *normal*, really, between us, and I don't know that I really believe that they will be again."

He sighed. "You may be right." He reached forward, brushed a tear off of my face. "So now what?"

"I have no idea. Voluntary amnesia?"

At least he laughed at that.

I shivered despite the best efforts of the heat lamps. "It's cold."

He cocked his head at me. "The water's warm."

"Thanks, have you told Al Roker that you're gunning for his job?"

"You're so funny. What I meant was, maybe we should take a dip."

"In what alternate reality is that observing the rules of voluntary amnesia?"

He smiled. "I didn't realize there *were* official rules of voluntary amnesia. Is there, like, a handbook or something? Maybe you could write me some crib sheets?"

I pushed him. "Keep it up, you're going in."

"That's kind of what I was hoping for, Maddie."

"My bathing suit is all the way inside. I'm way too lazy to go get it," I said. I also didn't really want to break the moment that we were having out here, alone, together. Inside it was still New Year's Eve, and Tyler was Spencer's boyfriend. Out here, we existed, however temporarily, in a bubble where I could have what I wanted and no one would get hurt. I definitely wasn't in any kind of rush to break the spell.

Tyler raised an eyebrow at me. "You don't *need* a suit to go in."

I flushed. I couldn't decide if my shock was genuine or put on. Either way, there it was. "What are you suggesting, Mr. DuPont?"

"I think you know what I'm getting at, Miss Takahashi."

"It's a bad idea."

"But it's a really *good* bad idea," he countered.

"My New Year's resolutions specifically forbid this sort of tomfoolery."

He shook his head. "New Year's resolutions don't start until New Year's Day. And it's not New Year's Day until you've gone to bed and woken back up again. Right now it's still New Year's Eve."

"That's a mighty technical line you've drawn, Mr. DuPont. It sounds like a pretty complicated system you're describing. Maybe you could, like, write me some crib sheets?"

He burst out laughing.

And then he kissed me.

First we were kissing, and I was protesting, and then his hands were in my hair, around my back, all over my body, taking off my dress, and I wasn't saying anything anymore, and then we were splashing in the Jacuzzi with the hot water matching my sizzling feelings, and even though it was, without a doubt, the Worst. Decision. Ever. (and not at all how I had hoped to ring in the new year) it was also the Best. Thing. I. Ever. Did. And I couldn't be sorry. The water bubbled up, tickling at my skin as Tyler devoured my neck and ran his fingers down my back, and when I opened my eyes to gaze at him, I could see steam rising off the surface of the Jacuzzi, which seemed completely and totally appropriate.

And then, suddenly, there was screaming.

Tyler and I flew apart. The bubble was burst, and reality flooded back in.

Namely, in the form of Spencer, standing over us, shock etched across her perfect features. Her mascara had run while she'd been passed out, giving her a sleepy, dark expression that amplified her fury to terrifying proportions. I recoiled, aware of the fact that I was completely naked underneath the bubbles and foam.

"*What* is this?" Her eyes were so wide that her pupils were drowning in whites. I'd never seen so much white in her eyes. It almost matched how pale her face had gone. "What are you *doing*?"

"I—" I didn't know what to say to that. What *was* I doing? Well, it was pretty clear, really. I just . . .

I hadn't planned on getting caught.

By now a small crowd had gathered, straining the deck's capacity. Through hot tears and the Jacuzzi's steam, I could barely make out Regan's look of incredulity.

"Holy crap," Kaylen said.

"Spencer!" Tyler sprang from the Jacuzzi like he'd been launched from a cannon and leaped back into his clothing, still dripping wet. "Spencer, baby, I'm so sorry. I can explain."

In response, she pursed her lips into a straight line, stepped forward, and shoved him backward. He stumbled and splashed back into the Jacuzzi, dousing me. I flinched.

Somewhere in the crowd, someone snickered nastily. "Dude."

Spencer turned on one heel and fled back inside. Regan shot me one last disappointed look and dashed after her as Tyler scrambled back out of the Jacuzzi and followed in their wake, water sluicing off of his body as he rushed back into the house.

I was alone again suddenly. Except this time, for real. It didn't matter that there were at least twenty people surrounding the Jacuzzi, eyeing me with varying levels of disbelief and hatred (though it did sort of matter that I wasn't wearing anything and wasn't about to get out of the tub until the throng dispersed; thank Dior for the foam skimming across the water—at least I knew they couldn't see anything other than my sad, pathetic face). None of them mattered at all.

Even *Tyler* didn't matter, I realized all at once. Never had. Not in comparison to the big thing. The Spencer thing. She is the only thing that matters, her friendship.

And that is clearly over. For good.

location: —
status: —
slut spiral: complete

Ty_It_On: is going to fix things, he swears.

1/2, 8:12 p.m.
privacy setting: private collection

SHOULD OLD ACQUAINTANCE BE FORGOT?

Survey says? Yes.

That is, if she's been caught red-handed with your boyfriend. Like I have, with Tyler. Spencer has definitely written me off of her list. Not that I blame her.

The ache in my conscience is pricking at my ribs like a knife's edge. And while Regan is being as neutrally polite to me as is humanly possible, no one else will even look me in the eye.

I basically hid out all of yesterday, alternately crying, sleeping, and feeling queasy. No one came in to check on me. I didn't go out looking for anyone. I didn't disappear into a hole in the ground, and I wasn't magically transported through time and space and deposited back, safe and sound, to my home, my Closet, my retreat.

Real life doesn't work that way, unfortunately. Dammit.

I occasionally heard muffled conversation, and here and

there I thought I could make out the sounds of Spencer crying, which made the knifepoint twist deeper, made me feel like I might be suffocating. But I couldn't leave my room, or even my bed, couldn't say anything to Spencer that might comfort her.

Seeing as how I was the one who had hurt her in the first place.

The plane ride back today was unbearable. I should have just bought a ticket and flown commercial rather than riding with Dalton and the rest of the crew on the Richmond plane. But I didn't have the energy even for that, and I certainly wasn't up to explaining to my parents why I couldn't fly home with Spencer. So there we were, together in a small, enclosed space, the pressure pressing against my temples and making my brain throb. Spencer tucked herself into a window seat and tilted away, outward, toward the sky. Regan flanked her, and Kaylen sat facing them, a self-appointed guard. She probably sees this as her big chance. Tyler stuck to the banquet toward the back of the cabin, buried in his portable DVD player, while C.J. busied himself with some game on his iPhone and Dalton smirked at me over the rim of a martini glass. I ducked behind an issue of *W*—twice the size of a regular magazine, thank Halston—and slipped on some oversize sunglasses. I didn't care if I looked like an ass, wearing sunglasses inside. I just needed some sort of shield, some barrier from the waves of hostility that were drifting toward me.

"Kaylen," Spencer asked, shifting slightly in her seat, "is that your water?"

Kaylen looked up from her iPod. "Nope, that one's yours."

"Great," she said, raising her voice. "Then I'll drink from it. Since it's *mine*. You can get your own."

Kaylen didn't say anything. Not that I blamed her.

"And thanks," Spencer added, smiling tightly. "I really appreciate a friend I can trust to know that what's mine is mine."

That was the closest Spencer came to talking to me during the ride. I don't even know what I would say to her, if she were willing to hear me out. What is there to say, after all?

I screwed up big-time. I'm a horrible friend. I can't believe I did something like this to the most important person in the world to me.

How can I fix this?

What can I do?

location: home sweet home, finally
days until school starts again: three
days until Spencer forgives me: God only knows

Madison_Ave: So . . . hi.

CaliforniaChic: Hey.

Madison_Ave: What's up?

CaliforniaChic: Nothing you don't already know about.

Madison_Ave: Um, yeah.

CaliforniaChic: So, how are you?

Madison_Ave: Uh, basically in a state of constant, agonizing guilt.

CaliforniaChic: That sounds about right.

Madison_Ave: So do you hate me too?

CaliforniaChic: I could never hate you, Mads. Besides, I'm the last one who should be throwing stones. I've made plenty of mistakes myself. I understand how these things happen. But that doesn't mean that you didn't mess up. Hugely.

Madison_Ave: Thanks. I wasn't sure how you felt, after the plane ride.

CaliforniaChic: Well, you know . . . I love you both. But I need to show some solidarity with the injured party until things calm down a bit. Spencer needs to know that I'm in her corner. Does that make sense?

Madison_Ave: Totally. And speaking of the injured party, how's she doing?

CaliforniaChic: Are you sure you wanna know? I'm not sure you'll like it.

Madison_Ave: I'm going to find out in school anyway. I'd rather hear it now. At least then I can be prepared. Hit me.

CaliforniaChic: Well, against the strong advice of counsel, she's decided to take Tyler back.

Madison_Ave: Huh.

CaliforniaChic: I mean, they're not, like, moonlight and roses right now, and I think he's still got a lot to prove, but she's going to give him that chance. I think she feels like it's the Kelly thing to do, to stand by your man despite scandal, to keep up appearances. Ugh. Makes me so mad. Like, he's just as much to blame as you are.

Madison_Ave: Thanks. I think.

CaliforniaChic: Sorry. But u know what I mean.

Madison_Ave: No, I know. I was kidding. Bad joke. But, anyway, yeah. The Kelly thing. She gets that from her mom.

CaliforniaChic: At least she's making him work for it.

Madison_Ave: I hope she makes him suffer.

CaliforniaChic: Well, I hope *you* don't have to suffer too much. This sucks. I hate that you both feel so lousy.

Madison_Ave: It's supernice of you not to take sides, no matter what.

CaliforniaChic: Well, I love you both, and I want us all back together again. If I stick close to Spence and help her through this, then maybe I can convince her to hear you out, try to patch things up with you—you know, later on, when she's ready to hear that kind of stuff.

Madison_Ave: Sounds good. The question is, how much later?

CaliforniaChic: Wish I knew. Only time will tell.

Madison_Ave: Time. Well, the good news is, I've got plenty of that at the moment. There's only so many hours a day a girl can spend buried in her sketches.

CaliforniaChic: Right on, for now, sister. That's the best thing that you can do.

1/9, 4:59 p.m.
privacy setting: private collection

WISH I WEREN'T HERE

Things that suck (in ascending order of suckage):

1. Not being able to check in with Spencer and Regan in the morning to compare outfits and update one another on every single detail of our lives. I mean, I used to be informed immediately even when Spence was just contemplating changing the color of her manicure. It's hard to quit that kind of closeness cold turkey.

2. Having to buy coffee on the way to school now that the student lounge has become enemy territory.

3. Dad's complete and total absence of late as he jets back and forth from Vegas and the West Coast, meeting with investors who want to open branches of his restaurants out there. Like, obvs, yay that he's doing so well, but right now I could really use . . . I don't know. Someone, anyone who kind of doesn't hate me at this exact moment in time.

4. Dissolving into my cello and designing not because I'm inspired, but because I have huge, yawning chasms of time that need to be filled and I no longer have best friendlies with whom to fill them. A cello makes for a lonely gossip partner.

5. The fact that Kaylen keeps inviting me to go to Saks with her for makeovers. Guess she's decided to make me her special project. Have I become that much of a pariah?

Which brings us to the final item on our Weekly Suck List Roundup:

6. The Spencer-size hole in my life.

And the deep, overwhelming fear that I'll never be able to make things right again.

location: the Bradbrary
MacBook: open
head: buried by screen

Toni_the_Tigress: might actually be feeling the eensiest bit of—could it be?—*pity* for our homegrown fashionista. Odd sensation, that.

1/12, 11:08 a.m., by Spencer Kelly

HELP A SISTER OUT

Pretty please, pretties?

If you're feeling charitable, come out and support the annual Sisters of the Main Line Runway for Hope fashion show! For reals, my mother and many of yours have put together this fantastic, first-class event, featuring gorj clothes, yum food, and tons of press coverage.

Are you ready for your close-ups, Bradfordians?

The best part? All proceeds go toward domestic violence prevention, so you get to have fun and feel good about yourself in the process, too. Consider it a perfect way to kick off the new year. After all, karma is a boomerang!

Hope to see you there!

Besos,

Spencer

2 RESPONSES TO "HELP A SISTER OUT"

QweenKayleen says: Ooh, so fun! Let me know if your mom is looking for any more models!

CaliforniaChic says: But of course, Spence. I'm all about the karma! (Now, if only I could get you to balance your chakras more regularly. . . .)

QweenKayleen: is practicing her catwalk strut. Tyra would be proud.

---

4 NEW RESPONSES TO "HELP A SISTER OUT"

QweenKayleen says: OMG, just heard that Chef Takahashi will be catering the event! Swankadelic! I heard he's opening, like, the hottest new restaurant in Vegas. He is going to be soooo huge (more than he is already, I mean)!

CatPower says: Also rumored that Mads's handbags are still going to be featured during the show. Guess it's going to be Takahashi Appreciation Day at the Runway for Hope, huh?

Toni_the_Tigress says: Hmm . . . that's mighty, uh, *charitable* of you, Spence, given everything that's gone down of late. Though I guess generosity of spirit is the order of the day.

GoldenGirl says: All true, ladies, I can confirm. But don't go mistaking me for Mother Teresa. All of these details have been in place for months, and the invites—including the list of designers—had already been printed. Duty first and everything. A Kelly always rises above.

1/14, 2:56 p.m.
privacy setting: private collection

ANGER MISMANAGEMENT

I entered the lion's den today. I violated the unspoken peace agreement.

This afternoon I dared to approach Spencer in the lounge.

I don't know what I was thinking; clearly, too many days with only the voices in my head for company have left my brain mushy and my instincts soft. But with the Runway for Hope show approaching fast, it just seemed like something needed to be said. I mean, my dad's catering her mother's event; my own designs are going to be on display. We're both going to be there, working the event, in a big way.

Honestly, I guess a part of me was looking for an excuse to talk to her. To break the ice.

Big mistake. Gigantic, humongous, *Vanity Fair* Oscar party–size error in judgment.

I've been making a lot of those lately.

I knew she'd swing by the lounge after lunch to pick up something energizing before physics class. So I hovered nearby as casually as I possibly could, pretending to examine the portraits on the wall of trustees. I figured it was a lost cause anyway. I didn't actually think she'd be alone when she walked out. I assumed she'd have Regan or Kaylen or (sigh) Tyler on her arm. And that would be that. She'd be surrounded, she'd swan by in a cluster, in a flash, and my moment would pass.

But that's not what happened.

Instead, Spencer strode out of the lounge, hair bobbing under a plaid headband, juggling her favorite Birkin of the season (the black patent snakeskin Kelly) and what I knew to be a grande green tea. It caught me off guard to see her relaxed and casual. She wasn't wearing that tense mask that automatically slides across her face these days whenever we happen to come within four feet of each other.

That slack in her face, that softened expression gave me a false sense of potential. I stepped forward.

"Spencer, hi."

She whirled to face me. "Madison." Her eyebrows knit together, first in confusion, then straight out in a line of anger, hardening with realization. The contours of her face were gone; she was all icy, stiff angles. The mask was back.

I kept going anyway. "I was thinking that, like, I know we've still got a lot of stuff to work out, you know, but since we're both going to be so involved in the whole Runway for Hope, maybe we should agree to, like, just put all that aside, at least for now—"

"Oh, is that what you think we should do?" She didn't snap it or snarl, merely said it in a calm, even tone. "What a fantastic idea."

I didn't dare reply. I knew then, by her unnatural calm, that I'd awakened a storm. Or worse—a dormant volcano. Spencer was totally about to erupt.

"I can't believe you just thought of that, all on your own, Mads!" she said, her voice growing louder as her eyes rounded. "That is, like, seriously brilliant!"

People were starting to notice, to perk up as they walked by. Most didn't bother to hide their morbid curiosity. I tipped my head down, feeling sick.

"I had no idea it was so easy. Do a heinous, horrible thing to your closest friend and then—*bang!*—just set it aside, whenever *you're* ready! How *convenient!*"

"I didn't mean . . . ," I mumbled, not bothering to finish the thought.

"No, seriously, that's awesome. I will just forget all about everything that happened, Madison. That's exactly what I'm going to do."

I allowed myself to hope for one nanosecond that she was telling me there was a chance for our friendship. But it took only that long before she opened her mouth to complete her rant.

"I'm going to forget all about it, Madison," she said, leaning in so close to me that I could smell her tea with each breath. "And then? I'm going to forget all about *you*."

location: the Bradbrary
status: forgotten
lesson: learned

1/15, 9:02 p.m.
privacy setting: private collection

RUNWAY TO REALITY

Regan came over tonight after dinner. My spring collection samples arrived from the atelier yesterday afternoon, and then I was stuck and couldn't figure out how to finish off a few of the bags. With some, it had to do with the embellishments; with others, the straps and the linings needed adjustments; and with a few, it was even an issue of whether or not their basic shapes were working. I was desperate, and *W* wasn't providing the inspiration I had hoped for.

Regan to the rescue. I cried into my cell phone, and she rushed right over after a strained dinner of steamed lettuce vapors with the stepmonster (clearly, Regan needed a lot of persuasion to leave that happy scene). She had some helpful advice, which she imparted over goat cheese nachos, licorice, and SmartWater (for the electrolytes).

"There's a reason you're repurposing the vintage materials, yes? I mean, each of these fabrics means something to you?" she asked, scarfing down a handful of candy and dusting the grainy nonsugar crumbs off of her hands and onto my bedspread.

"Well, yeah, that is the point of the collection."

"So I think you just want to be sure that each piece has some unique twist but also retains some element of the original source. I don't know. Like, with this one—" She grabbed at a handkerchief hobo I'd created from a 1920s Hermès scarf. "So, okay, it's from the flapper era. And you gave it a seventies shape, which is awesome. But is there a detail you could add that would evoke both eras at once and tie them together?"

I pursed my lips, considering, and then clapped my hands together. "Fringe!"

Regan grinned. "Perfect!"

I hugged her. "You rock." I pulled back and rubbed at my cheek. "And you need to wash your hands and face. And give it a rest with the Sour Cherries." I may not love wearing candy on my face, but I do adore Regan. And she was a big help. Just having her there, rubbing sticky crud all over the surfaces of my bedroom, was a huge morale booster and got me back in the designing groove. But there was still something missing.

Or should I say, some*one*?

Three guesses who.

Yup: Spencer.

Regan says she doesn't think Spencer really meant what she said yesterday. That she'll come around eventually. But since Spence isn't talking to me directly, I have to take her words at face value. Which means that right now, she's still out of my life.

location: the Closet
collection: coming along
missing muses: exactly one. At least I still have my collection
to keep me busy. I honestly don't know what I would do if
it weren't for that.

1/17, 3:43 p.m.
privacy setting: private collection

REALITY BITES

This morning I went to Spencer's house. And paid for it in thick, ugly, nonrefundable chunks of ego. Clearly, at this point, I'm just looking for ways to feel even more pathetic.

I woke up feeling drunk from the aftereffects of talking fashion with Reegs. That was clearly what sent me down this ill-advised path. But I had a plan, you see. One that Spencer would be helpless to resist—a packet of Spencer kryptonite. I tell you, the collection was fail-safe. Or so I thought.

I gathered up a mother lode of her favorite things, including but not limited to: a special foreign edition of *Philadelphia Story* with all sorts of cool extras and extended scenes not available on the original DVD, a pint of Smooch dulce de leche gelato, a bottle of Essie Mademoiselle nail polish, a tube of Fresh brown sugar lip balm . . . and the Glamourista hobo sample that Regan and I had finessed last night. It was supposed to be one of the bags featured in the fashion show, yeah, but I also knew that, style-wise, it was right up Spencer's alley: old-school glamour with a twist. I hated to give up one of my favorite pieces before the event, but it was going to the right home, I was sure.

I stuffed all of the goodies into the bag and tied it all with a pretty satin bow, then headed on over to the Kelly manse. I must admit, I was not at all prepared for what I encountered there. Though I probably should have been.

Upon allowing me inside, Carmelita assured me in hushed tones that "Miss Spencer is not home." Which all would have been perfectly well and good had it not been for the look of abject, wild-eyed panic on her face as she broke the bad news to me. And had it not been for the jubilant shrieks of laughter emanating from the general vicinity of the game room as we stood there, surveying each other awkwardly.

Those shrieks were Spencer shrieks. With a side order of Regan. There was no mistaking either of them. And they were clearly at the Kelly home. Together. Having fun. While Carm was under strict orders to keep me off the guest list.

"So sorry," she repeated, her voice echoing off the parquet floors of the foyer. "Miss Spencer is not home."

"Right," I said. "Of course she's not."

I shot a look toward the staircase, in the direction of the game room, contemplating making a run for it, bursting in on Regan and Spencer and forcing them to include me in their weekend girl time. But even I hadn't stooped that low.

Not yet, anyway.

"Of course she's not home," I repeated, the buzzing sound in my ears doing little to conceal the audible proof that I was being lied to, being shut out, being written off. "So, um, can you just leave her this"—I thrust the bag of gifts toward Carmelita, who stepped forward and accepted it—"and, uh, tell her I stopped by?"

Carmelita surveyed me, pity in her dark eyes. "Of course, Miss Madison," she said, taking the bag from me and tucking it under the marble-topped rosewood entry table. "Of course I'll tell Miss Spencer you came by."

And then, as if I didn't know the way on my own, hadn't been coming and going from this place since I was barely big enough to walk, couldn't see the door that was directly behind me, she kindly showed me out.

location: home, again
humiliation: complete
Glamourista collection: down by one piece. But it was for a good cause.

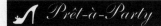

1/20, 6:08 p.m.
privacy setting: private collection

HOW NOT TO DEAL

Here's a scenario (totes hypothetical, natch): Let's say that you've done something completely grotesque and sluterrific, such as, oh, I don't know . . . sleeping with your bestie's boyf. For example.

She's no longer talking to you, and everyone in school is gossiping about you, and the boyf in question won't even make eye contact when he sees you walking down the hall, he's being kept on such a short leash.

So, you're all afflicted with depressyitis and going nuts from having no one to talk to, and there's a big fashion show coming up that you can't even get psyched about because your former bestie would rather stab herself in the eye with a straight pin than congratulate you on your very first runway collection.

There are several things that you can do in such desperate times:

1. Lose oneself in schoolwork. This option is neither particularly effective nor fun.

2. Embrace a new hobby. For instance, I've taken the art of creating frozen dessert concoctions to an entirely

new level. I'm pretty sure I've tried every possible Smooch gelato/topping combo.

3. Cultivate new friendships. If you can find anyone who will still talk to you who isn't also known for flashing people when drunk on three White Russians and a lemon drop shot and looking to use you as a springboard for her own power play, that is.

And even if I *was* itching to spend more time with Kaylen (which, ps: I'm not), all the girl wants to do is whine about how torn she is between Spencer and me. Apparently, our little falling-out is just eating her up inside. But not enough to SHUT. UP. ABOUT IT. Gah.

Note that I did not suggest summarily turning to a life of crime. And yet.

The worst part about it (although, to be honest, it's all pretty bad) is that the lonelier and more desperate I get, the sloppier I get too.

I came close again today. Close to getting caught. It's like I've reached inside my own soul and slammed on the self-destruct button with everything I've got. And the big guy, that Unnamed Designer in the Sky, heard the distress signal, looked down, and went, *Sure, we can do that.*

I wasn't planning to swipe anything at Jasmine—really, I wasn't. Lifting takes a certain amount of energy that I just haven't been able to muster of late. But then I saw it, a Tocca mulberry sequined cosmetics case, and I knew that Spencer would love it.

I could have waited, of course, until the salesclerk was off checking on stock for some underfed, husband-stealing former nanny. But that's not the way this whole grabby-sticky-pinchy thing works with me. Instead, I quickly checked the case for security tags, ripping out a sticker I found on the inside lining. As I was about to drop the item into my oversize purse, I noticed the clerk glance furtively to a corner of the wall. It didn't take me long to follow her gaze, and there it was. So obvious, really.

A security camera.

A security camera on which I was *most* definitely captured pawing at the makeup bag and ripping tags and whatnot and generally being a menace to society.

Pathetic, right?

I quickly deposited that cosmetics bag right back where I had found it and walked out of the store. My heart pounded the entire time, but no alarms sounded and no one stopped me from leaving. So I just assumed that whatever was or wasn't caught for all eternity on film had no bearing on my own presumed innocence.

Phew.

Spencer would have *totally* loved that makeup bag, by the way. If I could only get her to acknowledge my existence, that is.

location: the family room. A shot of vintage MTV programming
   is what this girlie needs.
pending arrest warrants: none, whee
reasons I have to grab a brand-spanking-new cosmetics case:
   zero. Zip. Zilch. And yet.

1/21, 3:28 p.m.
privacy setting: private collection

KNOWLEDGE IS POWER

If I could only figure out how to use it for good.

So, Regan clearly either took pity on me or somehow managed to wriggle away from Spencer for a few brief moments this afternoon, because she made plans to meet up with me in the library to do some research for lit class. I suspect it may have just been an excuse to catch up, since neither of us really needs to log any extra library time, but as excuses go, I was on board.

Have I mentioned it's been kind of lonely of late?

So, yeah. The Bradbrary. Maybe it's Regan's secret meeting place of choice, because when I finally spotted her, she was at a table in a corner, talking urgently with an intense-looking Jeremy Brown. (And when Jeremy Brown does "intense"? Let me tell you; it's intense.) I wasn't trying to eavesdrop, swearsies, but they were talking so seriously that I didn't want to intrude. So I quietly chilled in the stacks, waiting for a break in the convo.

How does that saying go? "Ignorance is bliss"? Well, it's probably true. But I wouldn't know right now.

"Look," Jeremy was saying, "it's not like I'm not at fault

here, but I don't feel great about being involved in someone's cheap revenge scheme. I would never have hooked up with her if I'd known about everything else that was going on."

"You think Spencer used you to get revenge on Tyler?" Regan asked, her forehead crinkling in disbelief.

"What else would you call hooking up with me days after she finds out Tyler's sleeping with her best friend?"

At that, I cringed. I couldn't help it. Not about Spencer and Jer, because, whatever—though it didn't escape me that if they had just gotten together before, none of this mess would ever have happened. No, my reaction was mainly because I still haven't gotten used to the idea of what I did to Spencer even though I'm the one who did it.

Does the guilt ever go away?

Never mind; rhetorical question.

"Okay, so maybe she wasn't thinking clearly," Regan said, her tone even and conciliatory, "but I doubt it was like an eye for an eye kind of thing. You know she still has feelings for you. I'm sure she's just as confused."

"Right," Jeremy said. He sounded disgusted, though whether it was aimed at himself or at Spencer, I couldn't tell. Probably a little of both.

"I should have known better," he said finally. "Whatever is going on between me and Spencer, she's still with Tyler. I'm the idiot who keeps losing sight of that."

"You're not an idiot. These things are just complicated," Regan said.

Reegs. So good with the non-judgyness. It's what she does, and she does it well.

"Yeah." Jeremy's voice was harsh and bitter. "And they just got *more* complicated. Thanks to Spencer's little games." He stood up and pushed away from the table.

"Jer—"

He turned and strode out, nearly plowing into me in the process.

"Sorry, Madison," he said, looking startled. "Didn't see you there."

"Yeah, no, it's okay," I mumbled as he kept walking. "I just got here. . . ."

As I settled in at the table, I caught Regan's questioning look and said, "My lips are sealed." She looked visibly relieved. She needn't have worried. Regan's the only real friend I have left at this point (Kaylen so doesn't count), and I'm not about to ruin that. Besides, the last thing I need is to get involved in someone else's drama. I have way more than enough of my own, obvs.

Still, though, now that I've had some time to process, my head is reeling. So Spencer turned to Jeremy in her time of need. And yet, she still isn't talking to me.

How does that saying go? Oh, yeah: Two wrongs don't make a right.

But then, there's still that adage about people in glass houses. Meaning, I have nary a Jimmy Choo to stand on.

location: the Bradbrary
status: adaged out
grass: still greener elsewhere

WonderBoy: definitely doesn't understand women. Or maybe he does, and that's actually the problem?
to: Madison_Ave@bradfordprep.com
from: Ty_It_On@bradfordprep.com
date: 1/22, 5:02 p.m.

re: Better Late Than Never?

Hey, Mads—

I'm really sorry that I haven't been exactly available lately. It's been really hard, ever since New Year's and everything that went down. But it's not that I don't care about you or that I don't miss you. I hope you know that.

I think about you a lot, and I'd really like to see you. Just to talk, you know? There's still some stuff I'd like to say to you, if you think you'd be willing to hear me out.

What do you think?

Love,

Tyler

1/22, 11:47 p.m.
privacy setting: private collection

A GLUTTON FOR PUNISHMENT

Sometimes I shock even myself.

I can't believe I fell for it. Tyler's "apology," I mean.

His e-mail stirred something in me. Maybe it was just a sense of righteous indignation, of needing to be validated. Of wanting to hear what exactly he still had to say. Or maybe it was just that self-destructive impulse that's been pulling at me since I first hooked up with Tyler at the Hollywood Ball. Whatever it was, I told him I was willing to see him. (Though, to my credit, I waited an entire hour before e-mailing him back. Girl power.)

He wanted to see me right away. Tonight. I said okay. The moment he walked through my door, I realized why he'd been so insistent in his e-mail. So sensitive. So "emotional."

He'd been drinking. He reeked of Scotch, which I discovered as soon as he leaned forward to kiss me on the cheek.

"Wow," I said, pulling back. "I hope you didn't drive here."

He shook his head. "Driver's waiting outside." He wasn't at the point where he was slurring his speech, but he was overenunciating and blinking a lot. I recognized this stage of inebriation. This was the *in vino veritas* stage. The stage that always gets the two of us into trouble.

I led him into the drawing room. Dad is on a business trip—London this time, I think—and Mom decided to say yes to drugs for the evening. She and Prince Valium have been in bed since nine. Good times. But at least that meant that Tyler and I could have some privacy.

What was I saying about getting into trouble?

"What's going on, Tyler?" I asked, settling into the ultra-modern, eco-friendly chaise.

"I miss you," he said, his voice breaking. He folded over into the couch and buried his head in his hands. "I messed everything up."

I sighed. "You didn't do it alone."

"Spencer's mad at me, you hate me—"

"I don't hate you, Tyler," I said. It was true, unfortunately. In a way, I wished I did hate him. That would have made things so much easier.

He reached into his coat pocket and pulled out his flask. The one she gave him for Christmas, the one I'd picked out for him first. He unscrewed the top and took a long pull. Then he looked at me. "She hooked up with Jeremy, did you know that? When we got back from Aspen."

I didn't say anything. Which told Tyler everything he needed to know.

He threw the flask across the room. It hit the marble edge of the fireplace, then bounced backward. Thankfully, he'd drained it first.

"I know she did it just to get back at me, to hurt me the way that I hurt her."

"Well, did it work?" I wasn't sure I wanted to know the answer, but I couldn't stop myself from asking the question.

"Hell, yeah." He looked at me like I had suddenly sprouted a second head. "Of course it worked. The thing is, I always worried that something like this was going to happen."

"That you were going to cheat on her and she was going to get back at you by having sex with an ex-boyfriend?" Because that would have involved either a mondo amount of foresight or way more self-awareness than I'd ever given Tyler (or any boy, really) credit for.

He shot me a look. "That she was still in love with Jeremy. That she'd get back with him."

Oh, that. "Well, she didn't get back *with* him. She got back *at* you." I decided to keep the part where I knew for a fact that she still had some lingering feelings for Jeremy to myself. I mean, why go there? I'd already caused more than my fair share of trouble for Spence and Tyler. Plus, I'd promised Regan to keep my mouth shut.

"Yeah." Tyler shrugged. "You know, I've been thinking about it, and I honestly do think that's why . . . well, that's why you and I got closer when we did. Because I always had, like, an attraction to you."

I glanced away. "I know. Me too."

There it was: the *veritas*.

"But I would never have done anything about it. I would never have gone behind Spencer's back. Until Jeremy came back. And I just had this, this *feeling*, like there was some unfinished business between them or something. And she was all 'friends' with him, and you were there, and . . ."

"And," I echoed sadly. I mean, that was pretty much it right there. In a nutshell. The history of how I'd come to be a backstabbing, boyfriend-stealing bitch. *And I was there.*

"Anyway." He stood again, and I rose with him, grabbing his flask and tucking it back into the interior pocket of his jacket. I smoothed his lapel and smiled up at him grimly. I couldn't believe that I had smiles of any sort left for him, but apparently, I'm a glutton for punishment.

"Thanks, Mads," he said.

"For what?"

"For letting me come by and be pathetic and whiny after I've made things so crappy for you lately."

"Oh. That."

"You're not even going to try to protest?"

"Things have been rather sucky. I'm not going to tell you otherwise."

"Right." He ran a hand through my hair. "Well, let's make a pact that we'll try to keep it friendlier from now on."

"Sure," I said, working hard to keep the tremble from my voice. "Friends."

Tyler leaned forward and wrapped his arms around me. I allowed myself to breathe in the scent of him, Scotch and all. Suddenly, I wasn't feeling like just friends. And I knew that I wasn't the only one.

Nothing good can come of getting all very with the vino, that's for sure. But it was way too late for second thoughts.

location: the drawing room
status: alone, now
friend count: same as it ever was. Tyler and I can never be just friends. Who are we kidding? I think we're going to have to stay away from each other for a while. But what else is new?

1/23, 1:09 p.m., by Regan Stanford

SOCIAL SHUTTERFLIES

Hey, Bradfordians:

Don't forget to come out for the opening of Jeremy Brown's photography show at the Independence Gallery. Tomorrow, Saturday, 5–8 p.m. Cocktails will be served (as if you needed another reason to show!).

The show is titled "Safari." Dress accordingly. I'm dusting off my leopard print Balenciaga as we speak.

Smile, people! See you there!

4 RESPONSES TO "SOCIAL SHUTTERFLIES"

Cap'nCrunch says: I've got the mosquito netting and the convertible Jeep! See ya!

QueenKayleen says: OMG, Jer. This is so awesome. I totally always knew you could do it.

Toni_the_Tigress says: Top-shelf cocktails, or what? I'm just saying.

Ty_It_On says: Gee, what a bummer that I can't make it. It's just tearing me up inside. But I've gotta rest up for a big date with Spence that night. Sorry, buddy.

CaliforniaChic: Hey, chickie.

Madison_Ave: Hiya.

CaliforniaChic: So, what time am I picking you up for Jeremy's show?

Madison_Ave: Oh, right.

CaliforniaChic: Oh, right, what?

Madison_Ave: It's just that I've been doing some thinking.

CaliforniaChic: Mads. I've warned you about that.

Madison_Ave: Ha ha. But seriously . . . You've been super awesome to me since everything happened in Aspen, and you completely rock, but I think you should go to the show with Spencer, not with me.

CaliforniaChic: Have you lost your mind, girlfriend? You know she and Jeremy are on the outs these days. Even if we're Not Talking About It.

Madison_Ave: Right, right, I'm on board with that. But still— they've been friends forever, no matter what's going down between them now. She'd never forgive herself if she missed his big moment.

CaliforniaChic: Wow. Taking the high road here, aren't you, Mads?

Madison_Ave: I thought it was about time.

CaliforniaChic: Hmm. She may take some persuading, though.

Madison_Ave: Some. Not too much. She really wants to go, when it comes down to it. You know that as much as I do.

CaliforniaChic: Well, if you absolutely, positively insist.

Madison_Ave: This is me. Insistent.

CaliforniaChic: OK, I'm off to do some negotiating, then. My work is never done. But—

Madison_Ave: No buts! Go make the call!

CaliforniaChic: Sheesh. I was only going to ask what you were going to do.

Madison_Ave: Don't you worry your pretty little head about me. I'll think of something. You know I always do.

1/24, 10:18 p.m.
privacy setting: private collection

BACK INTO AFRICA

I wasn't kidding when I told Regan I always manage to think of something to do. In this case, it involved doing what I could to repair things between Jeremy and Spencer. If I know her, the tiff with Jeremy has been eating her up inside.

My little fantasy about Speremy and Myler coupling off and riding into the sunset may have been utterly dashed, but I still knew Spencer inside and out. And I wanted to help get her a little closer to something that I knew would make her happy.

I waited until I knew Spencer had most likely come and gone from the show (Tyler had already announced that he had plans with Spence later that evening—sob—so I assumed that if I hit the gallery toward the tail end of the opening, I'd be safe). I donned my best "art geek" outfit: a simple but sophisticated black cashmere sweaterdress, spiced up with fluted sleeves and a rockin' pair of thigh-high purple suede scrunch boots. I traded my usual contacts for my tortoise-shell square-framed glasses, lined my eyes in a deep eggplant shade, and pulled my hair back into a supersleek low pony. I checked myself out in the Closet's three-way mirror.

Awesome. I *so* looked the part. I practically deserved my own art show.

I got to the gallery around seven thirty, and though there was a decent crowd gathered, things were definitely winding down. Which was perfect, for my purposes. Ulterior motives? *Moi?*

Never.

I waved hello to Professor and Mr. Brown, who were doing

the adorable doting parents thing, standing off to one corner and waxing on about Jeremy's photography while friends of theirs wandered to and fro. It made me nostalgic for a brief moment; Dad and Mom always attend my cello recitals, sure, but it's been ages since I've gotten any positive parental reinforcement. They've both been a little preoccupied recently.

Poor little Mads, right?

Jeremy himself was holding court in front of the centerpiece for the exhibit: a five-foot by four-foot black-and-white extreme close-up of a Kenyan shopkeeper talking to a young American traveler. Something about the lighting of the shot split the image directly in half, showcasing the photonegative quality of each figure. It was still and quiet but powerfully expressive.

Kind of like Jeremy.

I watched him talk at length with an art critic from the *Philadelphia Inquirer,* and I waited until he was free again before heading over to say hello.

"Wow," I said, coming up behind him. "Jer, these are amazing. I knew you were talented, but I had no idea how much."

"Thanks," he said, almost shyly. "Dad knows the gallery owner, which is how I even got the show. I mean, it's not like I'm some world-renowned—"

"But you will be," I insisted, cutting him off. "Don't sell yourself short. Anyone buy any of your pieces tonight?"

"Actually, yes." He grinned in extreme disbelief. "Looks like I've got at least a few people fooled."

I rolled my eyes. "What is this modesty? I thought the low student-to-teacher ratio at Bradford Preparatory School 'fosters a unique sense of self-esteem in today's adolescents.'"

Jeremy smirked.

"Anyway," I went on, hoping I sounded casual but suspecting that that was fairly unlikely, "who all came by? From school, I mean?"

"Oh, a few people, I guess," he replied, running his fingers through his hair. "Kaylen, Camden, C.J., Caitlyn . . . We have a lot of people with 'C' names in our class, huh?"

I grinned. "What about the 'R' and 'S' names?"

Jeremy shook his head, mock glaring at me. "Subtle, Mads. Very subtle. Yes, Regan's still here, somewhere, and Spencer came by. They were the first ones here, actually. Even before my parents."

"And how was it?"

"With Spencer, you mean? Well, things are a little weird between us right now."

"But still, the fact that she came? That's huge, wouldn't you say?"

Jeremy shrugged, noncommittal.

"Oh, come on," I insisted. "Stop playing it so cool. She is clearly your biggest fan, totally supportive, and totally in love with your work. Whatever drama you guys may have, that's the most important thing. The friendship."

"I know you're right," Jeremy replied, sighing, "I just wish sometimes that things were easier. Less complicated."

"You and me both," I said. I must have sounded wistful, or even a little bit pathetic, because he reached out and pulled me into an awkward, jokey headlock/hug hybrid.

It was completely goofy and utterly platonic, and yet, somehow?

Just what I think we both needed.

location: the Closet
status: headlocked and clearheaded
intact friendships: still a handful here and there

1/26, 10:49 a.m., by Spencer Kelly

MODEL BEHAVIOR

You can talk the talk, but can you walk the (cat)walk?

We'll soon see.

Announcing the Bradfordians who will be joining yours truly in walking in the Runway for Hope fashion show a week from this Sunday:

Regan Stanford

Kaylen Turner

Antonia Barnes

Caitlyn Pierce

Camden Barrett

Hailey Foster

Let's show those professionals how it's done, shall we, girls?

Tomorrow night: a meet-and-greet at my place for all of us to mingle with the designers. Attire is informal (read: cocktail).

Get ready to strut your stuff!

Besos,

Spencer

3 RESPONSES TO "MODEL BEHAVIOR"

Cap'nCrunch says: Who's fiercer than a Bradford girl?

QweenKayleen says: Nobody!

FilthyRich says: Hotties rockin' the haute couture? I'm there, yo. Front row.

1/27, 11:01 p.m.
privacy setting: private collection

THE STORM BEFORE THE CALM?

At least, I hope that's what this is. It would be ultrafab to know that there was a calm up ahead, on the horizon.

The good news is: I finally finagled my way back into Spencer's house, as one of the Runway for Hope designers featured at the Kelly meet and greet.

The bad news is: Spencer still isn't having anything to do with me. Actually, no, wait—the bad news is way worse than that. Had she simply ignored me, that would have been a huge improvement. As it was, she managed to shoot daggers at me with her eyes throughout the night.

I arrived at seven on the dot, as per the invite, cocktail-clad in one of my own designs and fully prepared to be nothing but professional. But when Spencer caught sight of me, she made a face like she had tasted some bad caviar and turned away from me before anyone else could notice the slight.

I did my best to mingle, giggling maniacally at everything anyone said (which, I must admit, was not always the appropriate response). The other designers, including my local fave, Marin Vose, were way nicer than a sixteen-year-old really has cause to expect. Which was refreshing, since the Bradfordians were taking their cues from their resident queen bee and mostly giving me the cold shoulder.

"Oh. My. *God*," Spencer hissed as I lay my samples across the dining room table. "Is that patent leather? How cute. It was so trendy last fall." She smirked at me.

I glanced up at her. I don't care what is going on with us; she was behaving more like Paige than like herself. Which isn't a compliment at all. I could see elbows digging into ribs and looks being exchanged among the other models. Regan gave me a sympathetic look. Not only was Spencer being nasty, but she was making the rest of the guests a little uncomfortable.

"Cutouts," Spence went on. "How retro. I think I saw something like that at the Gap last week."

I couldn't let that slide. "Since when do you shop at the Gap, Spence? Were you slumming it or something?" I heard a few sharp, nervous giggles before she cut them off with a queen bee glare, and I immediately felt bad. "Never mind," I mumbled, excusing myself from the sad little game of one-upmanship. "I, um, have to refresh my drink."

I wandered off to the bar, which was temporarily unmanned. I mixed myself a stiff Absolut and tonic, leaned back, and took a huge sip.

"Thirsty, dear?"

I looked up to find Mrs. Kelly standing above me. I wasn't concerned about my cocktail; she isn't the type of parent to freak over a little underage drinking. It's more that I was embarrassed to be discovered hiding out from the party. Not exactly the professional image that I wanted to project.

"I guess the pressure of putting together the collection in time for the show kind of got to me." It was the best answer I could come up with.

"Well, you've done a wonderful job," Mrs. Kelly said, patting me stiffly on the shoulder. She isn't exactly a warm or gushy type, so for her, this was high praise. And, I might add, much needed. But it wasn't quite enough to undo the seething resentment Spencer had been throwing my way all night.

"It just seems . . ." I wasn't totally sure how to phrase this, but given Spencer's absolute refusal to thaw, it seemed important to try. "Like maybe you already have enough to show? For the fashion show? So maybe I don't need to show?" I began to think I needed to broaden my vocabulary a bit, to get away from the word "show." Sheesh.

"What are you saying, dear? You don't want to be in the show?"

There it was again. That word.

"No, it's not that," I stammered. "Of course I want to be in the show. It's such an amazing opportunity. But the meet-and-greet seems pretty crowded. So maybe you guys don't need me. Like, I wouldn't be offended or anything if you didn't want me in the . . . if you didn't need me."

Mrs. Kelly squinted at me, like I'd maybe begun to speak in a foreign language and she hadn't quite caught what I was saying. Then she took a deep breath.

"I'm not sure I understand what the source of your concern is, Madison, dear, but we've paired your collection up with an amazing local designer who is expecting to use the bags as accessories. So I'm not at all concerned about your participation, and in fact, at this point, I'm counting on it. If you were to bow out now, we'd have to make a last-minute replacement. And that simply won't do."

"No, of course not." The last thing I needed was to piss off the coordinator of my very first runway show. The only reason I'd even suggested dropping out was because it was obvious that Spencer couldn't stand the sight of my face these days. I had hoped that being forced together for this event might thaw her out, but she's like a human Popsicle. Britney Spears will resort to her natural hair color before Spencer mellows out.

No matter. The show must go on.

Sigh.

location: bed
status: sigh
collection: "last fall," "retro," and "Gap-esque"

1/28, 2:09 p.m.
privacy setting: private collection

NINE TENTHS OF THE LAW . . .

. . . is possession. Meaning that what used to be *our* sofa in the Bradford student lounge is now the sole province of Spencer and Regan. Mind you, Regan does look awfully sympathetic from her perch.

Still, though.

Nine tenths.

location: the Bradbrary
possessed of: zero tenths
my kingdom for: a love seat, a chaise—a footstool!

1/28, 11:03 p.m.
privacy setting: private collection

(WRONG) NOTE-WORTHY PERFORMANCE

Note to Dad: Asking me to perform at your chichi little dinner party last-minute? When I haven't seen you all week and have a lot on my mind and honestly, didn't even know you were getting home from San Fran today?

Not so cool.

Though I guess, in the end, I got you back by playing like a drunken walrus. Your guests sure looked like they were enjoying the concert. Not.

The one person who seemed to get a kick out of my pathetic display? Spencer Kelly.

Oh, yeah—that was an extra-awesome surprise, coming home to find that she and her parents were guests at your last-minute event. I particularly liked the part where Spencer sat right up front and glared at me through every sour note, every miserable stroke of the bow. I think she put a hex on me to make me screw up.

And, man, did it work. I was so distracted by her presence, I went from prodigy to pathetic in moments.

Bonus: you coming up to me after the guests had left and assuring me that you were "disappointed in my performance." Because I couldn't possibly have guessed that from the frown on your face as I played.

By the way, Dad—the one thing *I* forgot to mention? I'm pretty disappointed in you, too, lately. Your performance as a dad? It could use some finessing.

Looks like you're no virtuoso either.

location: bed
status: disappointed, all around
cello: retired to its case for the time being

 *Prêt-à-Party*

1/29, 11:23 a.m.
privacy setting: ready-to-wear

FELIZ CUMPLEAÑOS A MI

Happy birthday to me
Happy birthday to me
Happy birthday dear Mad-i-son
Happy birthday to me!
And many moooooore.

Sure wish I had my best friend to celebrate with.

location: the Bradbrary
status: older
birthday plans: flexible, should the pleasure of my company
   be requested

COMMENTS (1):

CaliforniaChic says: Happy happy, girlie! Let's meet up and head to Smooch later. I have a gift for you—including some hair accessories from my fave LA shop that I *know* you're going to heart! Yay! XOXO

1/29, 1:56 p.m.
privacy setting: ready-to-wear

FELIZ CUMPLEAÑOS A MI (STILL)

The birthday plan has been confirmed: Regan, Kaylen, and my bad birthday self, Smooch, after last period.

(There's room in the car for one more. And I do not mean Dalton, even though he offered. Not even.)

location: the hallway
status: Prêt-à-Party, birthday edition
mood: older

1/29, 7:56 p.m.
privacy setting: private collection

FELIZ CUMPLEAÑOS A MI (RECAP)

Gelato: yum.

Gifts: fun (perfectly funky Me&Ro earrings from Reegs, a stylish sketchbook from Kaylen that I happen to know she special-ordered from a French papeterie).

Girls: adorable. Even Kaylen (I'm really not in a position to criticize).

And yet.

Spencer: absent.

location: the kitchen
menu: a fresh-packed pint of gelato from Smooch. YUM.
accessories: to die for

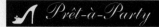

1/29, 10:01 p.m.
privacy setting: private collection

FELIZ CUMPLEAÑOS A MI (NOT)

I can't believe she didn't call.

location: the Closet
birthday: almost over
best friend: MIA

1/29, 11:59 p.m.
privacy setting: private collection

FELIZ CUMPLEAÑOS A MI (FINALLY)

All right, then. Now *that's* what I call a birthday surprise. No, Spencer didn't have a sudden change of heart.

But her boyfriend did.

I know, I know—but I deserved a little pick-me-up, even if it was in the form of Tyler, bearing a beautifully wrapped gift.

I didn't waste time protesting his visit. This birthday girl has spent too much of her special day feeling sorry for herself. I think I deserved whatever brief flash of joy his visit (and his prezzie) brought. I clawed the box open and gasped.

"Cartier?"

"It's a love bracelet," Tyler confirmed. "White gold. I thought you'd like it."

"I *love* it," I assured him, slipping the slim cuff onto my wrist and admiring the way that the interspersed diamonds caught the light. "Ha. Get it? I *love* it?"

"That's hilarious," Tyler said dryly.

"But . . ."

Tyler stepped closer and held my wrist up, giving himself a better look. "It's gorgeous. Like you."

"Thanks for coming by," I said. "I had . . . well, kind of a hard day."

"I had a feeling," he admitted. "And I wanted to show you that no matter how messed up things are, my feelings for you are totally and one hundred percent real. See? Smell my breath. No booze. I'm completely sober. This isn't a booty call."

He was saying all of the things that I needed to hear.

And he was leaning his face really, *really* close to my own. And in that moment I thought, *To hell with Spencer.* Twelve years of friendship and she couldn't even smile at me on my *birthday*? "So does that mean . . . ?" I let my voice trail off suggestively.

"Yes?" Tyler's eyes twinkled encouragingly.

"Does that mean we won't be having any booty? Because that seems like a waste of a perfectly good visit."

"It does, doesn't it?" Tyler asked, squinting and pretending to consider this perspective. "Especially since you're the birthday girl today."

"Birthday booty. It's only right." I tilted my head up and kissed him squarely on the lips.

Maybe I'm going to hell. Make that almost surely. But at least I'll have fun on my way there. And at least I ended my less-than-perfect birthday with a bang.

location: bed
wrist: still adorned
birthday: in the end, not too bad, actually

1/30, 2:54 p.m.
privacy setting: private collection

SCARED STRAIGHT

Not only is Spencer not noticing any new jewelry on my person, but she's also still doing her best impression of a person who absolutely hates my stinking guts.

I decided to circumvent all of the nastiness by stepping out to lunch for the afternoon, but instead of eating, I decided to do a little window-shopping. I thought I'd stick with the classics and wandered back to Jasmine. It was delightfully uncrowded at lunchtime on a weekday, save for a handful of trophy wives pawing through the one-of-a-kind silk lingerie displays. I wondered if they, like me, were grasping at straws, grabbing at sexy, silky diversions that might never even cross the path of whomever they were intended to impress.

I took a handful of slips, camisoles, and panties into the fitting room with me, scanned them quickly for security tags, and dumped them into my oversize Gucci satchel.

But I guess I wasn't vigilant enough.

As I stepped out of the store, a shrieking alarm sounded, piercing the calm ambiance of the sales floor. An impossibly skinny girl with a waist-length curtain of chestnut-colored hair stepped toward me.

"Miss?" she asked, the edge in her tone unmistakable. "You're going to have to come with me." She escorted me into the back room and, amidst my teary protestations, called the police.

The *police.*

There was no way out of this one. I'd officially gone too far.

The officers who arrived on the scene were a study in contrasts, almost caricatures of themselves. One was a short, portly man. His partner was a tall, slim, and thoroughly androgynous woman. They immediately lapsed into the "good cop, bad cop" routine.

"Miss . . . Takahashi, is it?" Tall/Good Cop asked.

I nodded silently.

"Are you a regular customer at Jasmine?" she continued as her partner glowered.

"Yes. I love their stuff," I said tearily.

"And is this your first time attempting to shoplift from the store?" Short/Bad Cop thundered, making me jump.

I don't know why they bothered to ask that question. Did they honestly think that I would confess to my previous steals? I may have been desperate, but I wasn't that dumb.

"Do you know what the penalty is for first-time shoplifters?" Bad Cop asked, squinting angrily.

"Um, maybe a fine?" I asked hopefully. "Community service?" I had a hard time believing I was going to be sent to juvie over a pair of underpants, but you never know, and this dude seemed ready to lock me up and throw away the key.

Little did he know that the worst thing he could possibly do to me would be to tell my parents what had happened.

"Community service," he scoffed. "Actually, Miss Takahashi—"

At that moment the door to the back office burst open, and the original shopgirl, the one who'd called the police to begin with, strode in with a tall, sharply dressed man at her heels.

The man stepped up to the police officers and spoke to them insistently.

It's possible that he thought he was being quiet. Discrete. He wasn't.

"I'm so sorry, officers," he began, dabbing at his forehead with an honest-to-Prada handkerchief, like a refugee from a Civil War period flick, "but there's been a terrible misunderstanding. Jasmine is not interested in pressing charges against Miss Takahashi."

"But she admits to having stolen the underwear," Bad Cop protested, causing me to squirm uncomfortably in my seat. I couldn't have tried to pinch something slightly less embarrassing? A pair of gloves or socks, maybe?

"Yes, but in fact, all of Miss Takahashi's *purchases* have already been taken care of. Her father knows she is quite busy and occasionally forgets to ring up items, and we have an arrangement for all of her shopping purchases to be put directly onto his account. So we are quite fine here, and Alison"—he shot a withering look at the shopgirl, who had the decency to look thoroughly abashed—"realizes her mistake in being so quick to notify the authorities."

Alison nodded, looking like she wanted to slit her wrists with a sterling emery board. I could relate.

"I'm *so sorry*, Miss Takahashi," Alison said, as she'd obviously been prompted to do, "and, of course, I want to thank you for being such a valued repeat customer of our store."

My head spun, even as the manager escorted the cops out of the store. I gnawed at a thumbnail, desperate to make sense of what I'd just heard. My father has an account on file at this store—and probably others—in the event of my shoplifting?

My father has known about my habit all along?

Clearly, he has. And he's never said anything, never talked to me or punished me or otherwise demonstrated displeasure or concern about this. All he did was all he has ever done: He took care of it in the easiest and most straightforward way that he knew how.

   With his wallet.

   I didn't know what to make of that. Of any of it.

   All I knew was that if I wasn't going to jail, I had to get back home.

location: the Closet. Nobody at school is going to notice if I take an extended lunch, except maybe for Regan. And she for sure won't say anything.

head: spinning

teenage rebellion: totes devoid of impact, evidently

1/30, 6:34 p.m.
privacy setting: private collection

A NEW LEAF

As in, I'm turning one over. Of the many things that I've done wrong since this school year began, stealing may have been the stupidest. *Especially* now that I know how bad I apparently was at it. Talk about humiliating.

This is the dawn of a new era, of a kindler, gentler Madison. Of a Madison who doesn't steal: not underwear, not sterling silver flasks, and certainly not other people's boyfriends.

Everything's going to be different now.

You'll see.

location: the Closet
self-discovery: complete
atonement: a work in progress

2/2, 7:08 p.m., by Spencer Kelly

YOUR DAYS ARE NUMBERED

Until the Runway for Hope fashion show, that is! Are you psyched yet? (And more to the point: Have you picked out your outfit?)

Here are some facts and figures to tide you over until the big event:

# of designers who will be showing at the RFH: 5 amazing professionals + 1 mere amateur

# of hours the show itself will last: 1.5

# of DJs involved in mixing together the music for the show: 3

# of makeup artists who will be on hand backstage to keep our models looking picture perfect: 2 per model

# of cases of Dom Pérignon ordered for the event: 20

# of tickets sold so far: 150

Donation required to snag a front-row seat: $10,000

# of front-row seats originally offered: 30

# of front-row seats currently available: 0

Hope you ordered your tix early, people!

2 RESPONSES TO "YOUR DAYS ARE NUMBERED"

CatPower says: So, are there six separate parts of the show?

GoldenGirl says: No. Note that I said, "one mere amateur"—she's just providing a few accessories for one of the true professionals.

2/4, 4:08 p.m.
privacy setting: private collection

A NATURAL HIGH

Who knew that there was a way to get that rush that normally comes from chocotinis, or from pinching things, or from smooching Tyler, without any of the icky side effects like hangovers, police lectures, and social Siberia?

I certainly did not. But I was glad to learn otherwise during the dress rehearsal for the Runway for Hope fashion show. Mrs. Kelly summoned us for what she called a "technical run-through," meaning that the models pantomimed catwalks and costume changes while the tech-heads on the payroll dealt with music and lighting.

Personally? I was in heaven.

To be perfectly honest, I would have happily died after checking in with Marin Vose and pairing up my fave handbags from my collection with her looks so that we were runway-ready. To be honest, it was hard to muster enthusiasm for any designer other than Vose after we'd had our fittings and she'd deemed my quilted clutch "reminiscent of an early Coco Chanel."

I like to be reminiscent of a legend, it must be said.

We were standing side by side, scrutinizing one particular look and hashing out the details of the model's potential runway makeup, when the backstage door flew open. Spencer swept in, a tornado of energy. She beamed a thousand-watt grin at Marin, being ultra careful not to allow even a stray glance in my direction.

But even Spencer's shunning couldn't bring me down. I was wearing my love bracelet, after all. And if there's one more thing I've learned over the last few weeks? It's that one definitely can't have one's cake and eat it, too. But even though I can't eat the whole cake, I can still stick my finger in the frosting.

location: the parlor. Doing a little bracelet-admiration mixed with self-reflection.
status: newly enlightened on all sorts of subjects
cake: uneaten. It's a whole catch-22 sort of thing.

2/5, 5:32 p.m., by Madison Takahashi

FASHIONABLY LATE

That's me, well past my deadline with your dos and don'ts for the major Runway for Hope event that goes down—*eee!*—this Sunday, but I assume you'll find the wait was worthwhile.

So without further ado, my friendlies:

DO:

1. Arrive on time. Fashion waits for no Bradfordian.

2. Wear one of the designers who's showing—or don't even bother to show your face.

3. Fall madly in love with one of my bags and come by Destroyed Girl later this month to buy it, duh!

DON'T:

1. Forget to accessorize. And I'm not just talking about jewelry. Remember, people: Double-sided tape is your friend.

2. Juice-fast the night before. The body is a complicated

machine, and the last thing we need is one of you passing out all over the runway just as the show gets under way.

3. Inquire about prices. How gauche.

3 RESPONSES TO "FASHIONABLY LATE"

Toni_the_Tigress says: Looking forward to dishing on your collection, Miss Mads.

QweenKayleen says: Thanks for the tips, Madison. Honestly, peeps? If you have to ask about cost? Really, you, like, shouldn't even be there to begin with.

CaliforniaChic says: Well said, Kaylen. Well said. As usual.

Madison_Ave: is going to rule the runway. Just you wait.

---

to: Madison_Ave@bradfordprep.com
from: GoldenGirl@bradfordprep.com
date: 2/6, 4:27 p.m.
re: You're Off the Hook!

Hi, Madison.

This is one of those good news/bad news sitches.

Here's the deal: One of the servants found your little bags and things and thought they were meant to go to Goodwill. Eek—can you believe it? (It's true what they say, you know—it's SO hard to find good help these days.)

So, obvs, the bad news is that I have no idea where your stuff is. Your collection could be who knows where by this point. Major bummer.

But don't worry—here's the good news: Leigh Cook from Cook and King is apparently branching out into handbags and accessories, and she has a line that she can show at Runway for Hope! So we're all good, we've got plenty of pieces to work with, and you don't even have to bother showing up.

Phew, right?

Besos,

Spence

Madison_Ave: has no words.

2/6, 8:01 p.m.
privacy setting: private collection

NO WORDS

Seriously. I can't even wrap my head around this.

location: my bedroom
status: speechless
mood: sans speech

2/6, 9:43 p.m.
privacy setting: private collection

ENOUGH IS ENOUGH

No more wallowing. The time for pity parties has come and gone. I can fix this.

I *will* fix this.

location: the Closet
status: determined
tape measure: in hand

to: GoldenGirl@bradfordprep.com
from: Madison_Ave@bradfordprep.com
date: 2/6, 10:14 p.m.
re: You're Off the Hook!

Hi, Spencer.

Thanks for your e-mail. You're right, that's a total bummer about my bags. Wonder how that happened, anyway?

But don't you worry. I'll be at the show, with a new collection, fully intact and ready to go. So there's no need to call in backups. My new collection will be even more chic than the original—swearsies.

And, Spencer?

I'm sorry. I know that what I did was totally unforgivable, but I'm going to find a way to make it up to you. Eventually. No matter how hard you make it.

And also: I miss you.

xx,

Mads

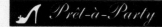

2/8, 11:01 a.m.
privacy setting: private collection

A STITCH IN TIME . . .

I have to admit, I wasn't sure I had it in me.

Of course, it wasn't only in *me*; Mom, Regan, and even Dad were big-time helps. When I explained the sitch, Regan came right over, and Mom scoured her closet for interesting fabrics that we could use to create a new collection. I still can't believe what she came up with.

In addition to several designer dresses, Mom gave me her wedding kimonos. Hers and Dad's. Mind you, she had to call him up and hunt him down in Vegas, where he was doing a second set of meetings with developers, and she had to work some serious feminine wiles to get him to agree to sacrifice such meaningful garments to the greater good. But whatever she said to him, it totally worked.

Once we had our fabrics, there was the question of how to pull everything together in the time allotted. I may be a design prodigy, but the truth is that I create most of my looks in my sketchbook and then scan them into my computer. A private seamstress at the atelier in Europe sews most of the actual samples for me.

But as it turns out, my design gene? Not a total fluke. Moms really knows what she's doing with a needle and thread. And she taught me everything she knew when I was a kid. I just needed a quick refresher.

We didn't finish until the wee hours of last night. Good thing Reegs and I are no strangers to all-night partying. I waited until nine this morning to call Mrs. Kelly and confirm the good news that we would be there with something to show after all. For her part, Mrs. Kelly sounded genuinely thrilled to know that I was still in the game. I guess she's still clueless about what went down between me and Spence.

I can only guess what Spencer's reaction will be.

location: the 'Bucks. Needing an extra java fix after pulling an all-nighter.
status: sleepy but proud
collection: Glamourista 2.0 ready to make its debut. So this is what *Project Runway* feels like. Squee!

FrontPaige: has a surprise in store for all of her old friends. Just you wait.

2/8, 5:14 p.m.
privacy setting: private collection

T MINUS FORTY-FIVE MINUTES . . .

. . . and counting, until my first collection makes its way down the catwalk.

Nervous, much?

Nah, not me. Ha!

Overheard backstage at the Runway for Hope fashion show as I arrived: Dr. Everett Cooper of the Museum of the Moving Image deep in conversation with Spencer's mother.

It seems that, as per the Sisters' request, he brought with him a dazzling vintage Oscar de la Renta cocktail dress worn by Grace Kelly at an Oscars pre-party back in the fifties. The dress itself is gorj, obvs, all bronze taffeta with beading at the neckline. Truly a showstopper, if you will, and it is going to be particularly fabu against Spencer's tawny complexion.

Dr. Cooper doesn't want anyone going near the gown except Spencer, seeing as how there are so many girls running around backstage trying not to get Vaseline from their teeth onto their outfits and duct tape from their boobs stuck in their hair.

If things weren't so wonky between myself and Spence, I would be thrilled for her. Wearing an actual Grace Kelly dress? She must be dying with happiness. Too bad she won't be squealing over it with me. But still, my own last-minute, rushed, cobbled-together bags will be strolling down the aisle with a little piece of history.

And now I have to breathe.

location: backstage
status: um, breathing
mantra: *Dolce . . . Dolce . . . Dolce*

3 NEW RESPONSES TO "YOUR DAYS ARE NUMBERED"

QweenKayleen says: Mads, your collection was totally amazing and stuff! *Mwah!*

CaliforniaChic says: Thanks for stating the obvious, Kaylen. So, Mads, when can I buy one of your bags?

Toni_the_Tigress says: Anyone else notice how a certain someone just may have wedged her way back into favor with her former BFF? Good thing, too, since they may need to combine their forces against a common frenemy.

2/8, 11:57 p.m.
privacy setting: private collection

EVERYTHING OLD IS NEW AGAIN

Here's the thing: Marin Vose? Kind of a beyotch, surprisingly enough. Okay, maybe I'm being too harsh on her; after all, she's really more of a perfectionist than anything else. And I can understand the strong, cloying need to have each and every piece properly accessorized before it heads down that runway.

But still. Bitchy.

Wait. Let me get this down in order. Set the scene.

Shortly after I arrived at the fashion show with my replacement bags (no way was I letting them out of my sight), I was grabbed by the elbow and *immediately* dragged behind a scrim by one Ms. Vose.

Her jet-black pixie cut stood up in stiff spikes, and she smelled of high-octane coffee. "Those," she said, gesturing to the bags in my outstretched arms, "are not the correct accessories."

"I know," I said, glancing at the clock. Thirty minutes until the curtain went up. "There was a slight problem, and I had to replace my original collection at the last minute."

Ms. Vose sniffed disdainfully as she glanced through the new bags. "Well, I don't appreciate the last-minute switch, but I suppose these will have to do. I don't have time to go through the collection and match these up, so—" She broke off and waved her hand as if to say, *Get it done.* As she turned away, she finished, "And please make any necessary adjustments to your collection so the audience will *not* know that this was rushed in any way. I will be back to check on your progress shortly."

Awesome.

Regan, who'd been hovering in the wings, hanging out in her slip and waiting for the stylist to put the finishing touches on her first outfit, shot me a sympathetic glance. I just shook my head, shrugged my shoulders, and sighed. There was no time for a pity party.

Backstage was madness of the veriest variety: half-naked models running back and forth trying to coordinate hair, makeup, and wardrobe, all while still in motion. Kaylen in particular was awful at this aspect of the job; I kept catching glimpses of her with one side of her hair clipped up in industrial bobby pins and false eyelashes wilting over her cheeks as some harried assistant attempted to stitch her into an outfit that was three sizes too small.

"If I, like, don't eat anything for the next hour or so, like, I should totally fit into this just fine," she was saying.

It was enough to make anyone crazy, but fate had more in store for us than veiled references to juice fasts and the like. I was down to my last pair of pants—a crazy, bell-bottom tweed that would be perfect with my patchwork frame clutch and that I needed to own the second this show was over—when I heard it: a shriek in the key of A minor.

"Kaylen! You! Look so! *Very!*"

I knew that shriek. I'd been dealing with that shriek for the last two and a half years of high school. And to be perfectly honest? While that shriek was off in rehab, I found that I didn't miss it that much.

Paige. Was here. Right now.

"OMG, Paige, you totally came and stuff!" Kaylen hobbled over, her feet bound together by whatever some poor design assistant had been trying to do to her before Kaylen's own personal Jesus had walked in the door. I couldn't help but notice that she wasn't *that* surprised to find Paige here.

"Mads," Paige said dramatically, stepping forward and beaming at me like she was Angelina Jolie on a U.N.-sponsored trip. "I heard about your pieces being in the show. That is so awesome." She hugged me tightly, pulling my body to her as I tightened my arms against my torso. "How great of Spencer's mom to have you here, right? The Kellys are soooo generous."

I froze in place, fixing a smile on my face as best I could. From over Paige's shoulder, I could see Spencer and Regan off to one side, taking in Paige's appearance. Regan was obviously less than pleased, and Spencer appeared completely uncertain, like she wasn't quite sure what to think about this former bestie who'd casually dropped in as if she'd been off on vacation instead of kicking a nasty drug habit. Both reactions, I acknowledge, were completely appropriate. They pivoted and darted off before Paige could catch them in a scary bear hug of death too.

I watched Paige warily as she walked off to continue making her rounds. Then I renewed my focus on making my new collection pair perfectly with Marin Vose's precious clothes.

In no time at all, it was six p.m., time for the show to start. The show runner, a tiny, Jack Russell terrier of a woman with a shock of curly red hair, darted around the backstage area barking, "Places, everyone!" into her headset.

I positioned myself at the edge of the curtain, where the models were poised on deck. Marin Vose's collection (and mine) was first. My heart threatened to pound out of my chest, I was so nervous. I looked up and down at the line of models, each one perfectly dressed, styled, made up, and carrying something that I had made. With my very own hands. That fact made this moment all the sweeter. I was going to explode from pride and fear and nerves right there on the spot.

I held my breath and managed to keep it together as the looks went down the runway. First was the fringed hobo, similar to the one that I'd made for Spencer, though this one was stitched from a sumptuous velvet my mom had worn to a charity ball last year. Then the crocodile satchel with the bamboo handles taken from sixties furniture. Then the tote woven from strips of a 1940s tablecloth. (Thank God I'm constantly saving interesting notions and fabrics for future projects.) A few more bags of various sizes and styles. And finally, the grand finale: the two oversize mix-and-match clutches made from my parents' wedding kimonos. I peeked past the curtains and into the audience. Dad wasn't there, of course (still traveling, what else is new?), but Mom was in the front row, dabbing at her eyes. She's not always the most sentimental person, so I knew from her reaction that I'd done well. And it wasn't just her. The entire audience was applauding now, grinning and whispering to one another. I even saw a few gestures that indicated they were mostly buzzing about *my* collection, not Marin's. They liked what I'd done. They liked my designs. They liked *me*.

It was a nice feeling. I'd missed that feeling.

"Fantastic work, Madison." I felt a hand clap down on my shoulder and saw Marin smiling at me. "You did a great job. If you ever need anything from me—a recommendation, advice, anything—seriously, just give me a call. You're amazingly talented."

Here I was, twinkling away backstage, while I could see Tyler, Dalton, C.J., and even Jeremy clapping and cheering from their seats in different parts of the front row. But this moment was fully my own. It felt good to be reminded that I did have some skills outside of boyfriend-stealing.

No. Scratch that. It didn't feel good. It felt *amazing*.

I looked up. Regan gave me two thumbs up and an enormous grin from her perch across the room at the hair and makeup station. The one thing that would have made this moment utterly complete would have been to be able to share it with Spencer. But obviously, she wasn't around.

I tried not to let the glowy feeling fade as I made my way back to the work area. After the "accident" that had befallen my original spring collection, I felt I should collect my bags from the models and move them to a secure location before enjoying the rest of the show. After all, I wasn't interested in remaking the bags for a third time to make Destroyed Girl's on-sale date.

Just as I was ready to watch the rest of the show, I heard it. It was soft, and honestly, I wouldn't have picked up on it, I don't think, if I weren't so well attuned to Spencer's distress signals after all these years. It was crying. And cursing. Very quietly, of course.

I turned the corner and poked my head behind a scrim to find Spencer shaking her head and investigating the skirt of the de la Renta dress.

More specifically, she was investigating a huge, honking hole in the skirt of the de la Renta dress. I couldn't help it. I gasped.

"Thanks," she snapped, looking up at me. "That's really helpful."

"No, I know, I mean . . . I'm sorry. I just . . . that looks bad."

She sneered. "Obvious much?"

I swallowed. "Do you need me to help you with that?"

Her eyes darkened. "No."

But we could both hear Jack Russell headset woman clomping back and forth, trying to get everything together for the grand finale. And as we both knew, Spencer *was* the grand finale. I paused, debating.

"My mother is going to *kill* me," Spencer said, running the metallic taffeta through her fingers. "I mean, this dress was picked specifically for me because she thought I could handle the responsibility."

"And that guy from the museum probably won't be too thrilled about this development either," I added.

"Are you *trying* to freak me out?" she asked, her eyes round and wet.

"No," I said. "I'm trying to convince you to let me have a look at that tear." I moved closer, waiting for her to protest, but she remained silent. "Look," I said, gathering the fabric up. "The tear is on the underside, in the crinoline. If I use the smallest needle, I can sew up the hole and no one will ever know."

She looked at me, doubtful, but infinitely hopeful. "Really?"

"Really really. Now, change out of it so I can work on it properly." She quickly slipped off the dress and stood there awkwardly.

I didn't wait for a further response and didn't bother making small talk while I worked. I hung the dress on a dress form and hunched over the skirt, deep in concentration. Spencer was quiet too, one part respectful of my need to focus and at least nine parts weirded out by whatever brief flash of understanding had passed between us.

"Okay, now put it back on," I said. She did, and I fluffed the skirt of the gown out so that it highlighted her miles-long legs. "Perfect. No one will ever notice."

"Really?"

"Really really."

Jack Russell shrieked for places again, and Spencer dashed off—delicately this time, so as not to ruin our handiwork.

Just as Regan finished her final strut (in a high-fashion black number), I watched Spencer march down the runway— tall, poised, confident—and felt proud, way prouder than I would have expected at how natural she seemed at modeling.

The audience erupted into applause, some even stomping their feet or calling out, and I knew that the finale had been as climactic as Spencer had hoped.

She stepped through the curtain, and her mother swooped her up into a rare embrace.

"You were wonderful, darling," Mrs. Kelly said. "Now get ready to go out there for the final bow."

Spencer glanced at me, then grabbed my hand impulsively. The final bow. We were taking it together. Regan joined us, and we vamped for the cameras.

Spencer let go of my hand and struck her supermodel pose. But it was okay. That one moment was more than enough. That one moment, coupled with *this* moment, where I could look out and see Jeremy, Dalton, C.J., and even Tyler grinning and cheering for us, all three of us.

That moment was everything.

And then it was over, and we marched backstage again.

"That dress certainly becomes you," Mrs. Kelly said, beaming at Spencer. "Now take it off before something happens to it."

And then something did happen. Not to the dress, but to me. Or rather, to Spencer-and-Me. At her mother's comment, Spencer looked up over Mrs. Kelly's shoulder and caught my eye. And she winked.

She winked!

Okay, so it wasn't like she'd offered me the last drop of her Crème de la Mer facial moisturizer or suggested that we trade Prada slingbacks for the day, but still, it was something. It was more than I'd had in a while. And I was going to take it. Happily.

Regan looked surprised but pleased that her two besties were starting to thaw their personal cold war. She gave me a quick hug.

"Yo, you were so amazing." It was Tyler, who'd finagled his way backstage and had now worked an arm around Spencer's shoulders. "You look crazy hot in that dress."

"Thanks," she said. She sounded as though she meant it.

The two of them wandered off, presumably so that he could "congratulate" her in private. Neither looked back at me as they made their way out of the melee.

And for once? I found that I really didn't mind. For the first time in a very long time, things seemed like they were starting to get back to the way that they were supposed to be.

And that worked for me.

location: home, bed, finally
first-ever show: a smash success
first-ever friend: coming around, I think. At last.

Ty_It_On: Hey, Mads. Sorry I didn't have the chance to talk to you tonight. Wanted 2 let u know that your collection was amazing. U rock.

Ty_It_On: Mads?

---

to: Ty_It_On@bradfordprep.com
from: Madison_Ave@bradfordprep.com
date: 2/9, 2:11 a.m.
re: Clarity

Hey, Tyler.

Thanks for your text. Sorry I couldn't get back to you right away. I was kind of busy. Doing some thinking, that is. And I've decided something. It's over.

For real.

I know we've said it before, but after tonight, after having a glimpse of what it would be like to have things back to normal with Spencer, I realized: Friends come first. They always should have, really.

This doesn't mean that I don't care about you or that I don't believe that you care about me. But if you meant everything that you said, you'll choose. Once and for all. And if you choose Spencer, well then, you and I will respect that. We won't hook up anymore, won't even flirt or do anything that Spencer or anyone else could possibly take the wrong way.

If you choose me? Tyler, if you choose me, then you have to really choose me. Like, break up with Spencer and give that whole situation time to heal, so that we can restart things on the up-and-up this time.

But I'm not counting on that. On you choosing me, I mean. You and Spencer have a real history, just like she and I do. I don't expect you to just throw that away. I'm sure not going to.

I just thought we should be clear on that.

Madison

Madison_Ave: knows now that a little clarity goes a long way.

2/9, 11:15 a.m.
privacy setting: ready-to-wear

RUNWAY RUNDOWN

Girlies! We have so much to address. For starters, the mere fact that I can address you both (and actually expect both of you to read it) is huge news. Spence, I'm so glad that we turned a corner last night and you don't seem to completely hate me anymore. I know it's going to take a while for me to build up your trust again, but I'm going to prove to you that you made the right call, I swear.

Secondly, we have the fact that the two of you *rocked it out* last night, and meanwhile, my collection was a hit. Natch. Because we three? Kill.

Thirdly, two words: Paige Andrews. Three letters: WTF? Is the wicked witch back for good, then? I noticed you giving her the brush-off backstage when she feigned remorse for her vendetta against you, Reegs. Sounds like the right approach. I find it difficult to believe she's had a complete personality transplant in the past six weeks or so.

And finally, what of that peck that Dalton gave Regan after we'd taken our final bow? Any chance it's true lurve? Yeah, okay, it was a kiss-kiss on the cheek, not on the lips, but *still*. STILL.

What can we do? This is Bradford, after all. When one drama closes, another one opens, right?

location: bed
status: content
drama: in flux, as per usual

COMMENTS (3):

CaliforniaChic says: OMG, Mads! What do I have to do to convince you that Dalton and I are so not? He's such a male slut—I saw him smooching *all* of the models backstage—just one more reason why I could never take him seriously. But as for Paige: correctamundo. Avoidance is the order of the day.

Madison_Ave says: But resistance, I fear, is futile.

GoldenGirl says: Oh, friendlies, but aren't you at least an eensy bit curious to see what her return stirs up? I'm not going to deny that I missed her a little in spite of myself. Regardless—with her back at Bradford, things are def about to get *way* more interesting.

Authentication Required

Enter username and password for
http://www.bradfordprep.com/BradfordWeb.html

User Name:

Madison_Ave

Password:

Franklin

Cancel   OK

http://www.bradfordprep.com/BradfordWeb.html

Brad

PREPARATO

WELCOME   ABOUT BRADFORD   ACAD

ADMISSIONS   ALUMNI   PAREN

News from Bra

MadisonAve

California_Chic
@GoldenGirl1 @Madison_Ave
Girlies! I'm so happyhappyhappy that you're waving the white flag again! Friendlies forever!

Madison_Ave
@GoldenGirl1 Aw . . . I tries, I tries.

GoldenGirl1
@Madison_Ave You SO saved the day at the fashion show, babe!

What are you doing?

ord
SCHO

CS STUDENT
BLOG BRAD

Bradford Preparatory
School

From:	FrontPaige@bradfordprep.com
To:	Madison_Ave@bradfordprep.com
Cc:	
Subject:	What's the 411?

Miss Mads,

Fabu seeing you at the show. We are WAY overdue for a catch-up sesh.

And SPEAKING OF, have you checked out Toni's blog of late? http://tonithetigress.blogspot.com/

What is the whatness that has our little California Chicklet so skittish these days? Backstory, if you've got it!

xx,
Paige

rd Prep

See the pics, scope the dish,
and read the other blogs at
BradfordPrep.com

You won't believe your eyes . . .

Photo © Michael Frost

Scandal never signs off. . . .

A BRADFORD NOVEL

Scandalicious

Turn the page for a sneak peek.

to: CaliforniaChic@bradfordprep.com
from: BadKarma713@gmail.com
date: 2/8, 8:44 p.m.
re: I so know what you did last summer . . .

. . . and where you are right now.

I know Bradford's favorite surfer girl loves to play laid-back, low-key, and laugh-a-minute. But you and I both know that you're not at all what you seem.

Your East Coast friends may not know the real reason you skipped town and left La-La Land behind, but I do, and it's only a matter of time before the truth comes out.

I've got the key. And I'm going to unlock that closet and watch your skinny little skeleton bones come tumbling out.

I'll tell everyone your secrets and watch you crash and burn.

Wait for it,

Karma's a Bitch (and So Am I)

Check
Your
Pulse

Simon & Schuster's **Check Your Pulse** e-newsletter offers current updates on the hottest titles, exciting sweepstakes, and exclusive content from your favorite authors.

Visit **SimonSaysTEEN.com** to sign up, post your thoughts, and find out what every avid reader is talking about!

Margaret K. McElderry Books

Simon & Schuster
Books for Young Readers

SIMON
PULSE